VAMPIRE DREAMS

A Collection of 32 Vampire Stories

By

Richard Reich

Dedicated to Mr. Stoker,
the art and legend of Dracula
in the 101st year

Copyright © 1998 by Richard Reich

ISBN-13: 978-0-6151-5668-2

Library of Congress Control Number: 2007908335

VAMPIRE DREAMS

Books By

Richard Reich:

————————

Word Songs

Dracula, The Reemergence

Vampire Dreams

Strange Manners

Strange Days

Contents

Contents continued...

VAMPIRE DREAMS

Hellfire

The fire burned so bright it scorched the fine hairs along her limbs and face... but she didn't get so close as to burn her sweaty locks. Auburn they were and the thought gave her pause for an instant, but only for an instant since the work was far too important to stop now. Her clothes were similarly undamaged as she tossed log upon chair upon crate upon useless plywood board into the cavernous blaze. She'd been lucky to find plenty of fire fodder in the mansion's basement and timber lying about in close proximity to the site she'd chosen on the large expanse of lawn behind the old house. As sirens began their steady peal in the distance she smiled knowing her work was now done. She would be safe, all of humanity may one day recognize her efforts and give her her due. Of course she couldn't care about that now. She might never care about anything again ever with what she'd gone through... gone through was a right choice of words. She'd been through hell, or at least severely abused.

It used to scare her to be out after dark especially behind the huge house with its shadow casting everything into pitch black nothingness all the way to the wood which were themselves the essence of blackness. Utter stillness, complete silence prevailed in the preternatural cold blackness of the forest beyond. As if even the birds and small creatures, usually of nocturnal ilk simply refused residence or sat within burrows in frightened silence until after dawn, only then venturing but a few brief hours for the necessary activities to sustain life a while longer. She hated the backyard and virtually ignored it when the gardener would report that a large tree had fallen or some wild animal had been found dead, or the nicest plants uprooted and left to die in the morning sun. After years of intermittent effort the gardener had been instructed to just let it go, allowing the yard to revert to an unappealing although more natural state. The front yard still yielded to his efforts so what the hell, her father used to say, no one needed to see back there. As long as we could keep the trees and vines away, the house would survive. She wondered though if there wasn't some threat, something living and potentially evil that wasn't somewhat more tangible than a tree or creeping vine... but time seemed to pass.

"Sweetness go out back to see if there are any new corpses today," my father would say half jokingly after having one too many drinks too early in the day. I knew he wouldn't say such things sober and the gardener, Ambrose, would immediately attend to the task if he discovered me out walking in the yard. Often I'd notice new rocks or boulders or things moved about as if some strange wild man had been keeping house outside and constantly rearranging the landscape to suit his tastes. What might the purpose be? Perhaps the gardener himself were mad but this was impossible as he went home at night and these things never happened by day for I occasionally observed long hours from my upstairs windows.

"I'll look for the poor wretches," Ambrose would say, and return a short time later with several misshapen bodies or parts of bodies that apparently suffered horribly at their deaths. Some days it'd be a raccoon, or a rabbit and a squirrel, sometimes several squirrels. Rarely a week or two would pass and nothing would be found except a small bird or two and I'd know we'd be due for something big, a deer or dog. Hopefully not the neighbors dog!

If I happened to see the animals piled near the porch ready for disposal I'd be sick and when I complained to father, "Why can't we just let them stay in the yard or call some agency to come get them, or find the beast whatever it is?" Then father would just shrug. "It's wild country this America. You have to expect this kind of thing when you live in the country. It was much the same in the old country too. It affected your mother the same way you know, in Transylvania. She would obsess and stay up all night thinking about her missing pets or the slain animals she'd see. She let it get in her blood and so she would go on hunts for some imagined beast, and at night! I tried everything to keep her home... books, music, dancing and even resorted to bondage at times you know but it was no use. She went mad."

"Yes father." I said, "She committed murder."

"That's right." he replied, "Tore into the town crier's neck like some wild animal of some sort. That's what you might call a night-watchman here."

"I know father."

"Well if it's any consolation, they say she had rabies. Maybe she'd been bitten while on the hunt. I could never understand it. I only know that I loved her."

"Yes father."

"And I was relieved she died before she could be put to death, a terrible thing to say but true. I never told you before but I couldn't bear to leave her behind so when we were ready to leave I had her exhumed so that she could make the trip with me. You were just a little girl at the time."

"You did father?"

"It may have been a mistake I know, but we held another small ceremony deep in the..."

"The woods!" I chimed.

"That's right sugar plum, I knew she would've wanted it this way. And it's funny but when I'm awake late at night from too much coffee or a storm batting a loose branch against the window I feel her presence as surely as you're here

11

with me right now. I'm not afraid to say that I like that feeling. You don't think I'm crazy?"

"No father, but the animals..." I muttered to myself as I went up the stairs to bed that night. That had happened several years ago now but I still remember how my father had said, 'What's crazy about a few dead animals now and then when you're with your loving mother... Someday you'll see it's for the best."

I wasn't sure what he'd meant at the time but I've seen my mother on several occasions since. Who else could it be, so late at night dressed in a radiant black gown and bending over father's bed, drinking it would seem from his neck... naturally I couldn't bring myself to speak of it in his presence. I know he would've denied it. But one morning I found Ambrose's lifeless body in the garden and it was too much. He probably stayed late one night, maybe at father's request, for I found that father was also ill, very white and looking near death. I told him about Ambrose and he said, "It's no matter, we won't need him now, it's me she wants. You know eternity and all that... we'll be together soon I think."

I did what any loyal daughter would do for a father turned... that 'word' from the old country, vampire, I think it is. He died, I helped him a little with a wooden stake through the chest and he and Ambrose are out there or they were until recently. They're ashes by now. The flames from the pyre are almost as high as the house. I've been feeding it for hours but it's hard to see being in the backyard. And for the first time I'm not afraid to be here at night. The animals will keep their distance and she knows how I feel about the whole thing. I think she'll leave me alone.

The Power of Gods

"Yea though I walk through the valley of the shadow of death, I shall fear no... evil, for thou art with me." One of the most oft ask questions of a vampire is about power... is it real, or like a drug trip? Too much, perhaps supernatural or like a Christian's faith in God... something that's always there to help him and guide him along his way, provided of course he has the good sense to choose the Christian way? But God is there helping to show the way should a man turn sinner and need redemption, or possibly punish him and allow him to see the error of his ways. Do vampires by chance have anything akin to that? You wouldn't think so. 'Hardly' some might say, 'vampires are evil... they live in the realm of night and darkness, and are inherently evil by nature.' Is it this essence of evil that is there with them, affording a protection or cloak of fear as they walk in their valley of shadows, of death? Possibly, but having personally known several vampires I'm sure it is only the weakest of vampires that relies on the ability to produce fear, such as encountering a criminal might cause. Rather I hope through this story to allow a glimpse of a powerful vampire, one who's strength maybe said to rival the power of the very gods themselves.

Back during the time of the early Roman Empire... after Caesar but before the lunacy of Nero there lived a man, who happened to be hiking in the country one day, in an area previously unknown to him as he searched the terrain

13

looking for more suitable grazing land for the herd of animals in his care. He happened upon a cave set amongst some trees and well hidden by a hillside. Finding it empty he decided to rest for the air was cooler and dry. He found matted grasses at the entrance apparently used by some animal for just this purpose and brought them inside. After checking briefly for ticks and other visible pathogens he determined the bed to be safe and comfortable. He promptly fell into a deep sleep. He didn't awake until the next morning. Though he was hungry, it was not hunger in the usual sense and for some reason his eyes had trouble focusing in the daylight. He was very irritated but could not walk more than a few steps without shielding his eyes. He fell to his knees and prayed. After a while he crawled back to the cave.

Once more in the cave he realized he was physically fatigued yet felt a certain inner strength of spirit, a confidence that had no reason to be there. He loved the feeling and allowed his mind to race with thoughts of joy and the overwhelming richness within his soul. Material possessions could scarcely compare to wealth such as this he thought, but in all probability the feeling would be changed after another day's fast if he could not leave the cave by then. The more he explored his mind the more he came to the awareness that this new feeling of well being, of inner strength was real and would always remain with him at least as a memory.

He was alive with wonderful new memories he never knew were there. He could stand up and debate the fat senators, whittle away their platforms and fray the fabric of their issues until they stood threadbare for all of Rome to see. He might even take on the Emperor himself with whom oratory elegance would no doubt be wasted as the Emperor's pleasures many knew inclined to only the vulgar sport of the Coliseum and the pleasures of the flesh almost to exclusion, or so it was rumored.

He wanted to rejoin civilization as soon as he could yet the cave held him captive by its comfort, by the strange change taking place within him. At the mouth of the cave the sunlight still made him cringe. He knew the animals would fare well on their own until his return even if it took weeks. That was a great thing about herding unlike the constant chore of manual labor work such as carpentry for which he'd been trained by his father. He loved his father but found it impossible to discuss anything except family religious matters with him. He could never tell him in so many words he didn't share the same love for crafting a fine piece of wood.

I thought it may be too much a mental stretch for most, too incredible for anyone to believe at first that someone from that early time could still be alive in this era... to narrate a story. So I chose a deceitful approach and apologize, but soon you'll see how I was able to survive and to whom I owe it all... my life and powers.

As I lay back in the cave and began recollecting my past with frightening clarity I also experienced a tremendous calm, which soon lapsed into peaceful sleep whose dreams achieved a lucidity to rival my waking thoughts. This time I knew there was the presence of another in the cave. I felt him come to me with my mind rather than any actual physical touch, but the contact was intensely intimate. I was of the surest conviction that my very soul had been reached but by whom I could not imagine or for what purpose I could not comprehend though I wanted to so badly. I concluded that I had indeed somehow managed to reach the heavenly heights and quite possibly Mount Olympus itself though I knew my body to be still there in the small cave. Had I died after just a day and a half from my fevered state perhaps a consequence of a previous poisoned draught from a stream, or a deadly plant or berry I 'd mistaken for the more familiar flora of the home range, it would not have surprised me as much as this...

I awoke early the third evening feeling strong and refreshed. I noted particularly peculiar was the fact I was not even the least bit hungry in the usual sense though there was an aching in my front teeth, two of which appeared somewhat more prominent then they should have been. I debated leaving the cave. I realized I possessed a new strength, so much stronger than my usual self. I began to have the strange notion I might just lift my wings and fly. Why I was suddenly imagining I had great wings I was not at all sure, but at that moment I was again acutely aware of another's presence in the cave. The cave was small and he could not likely have entered undetected. He must have been waiting there some time yet strangely I did not feel alarmed. Similarly he wore a common shepherd dress though I noted the sandals were well made, impressive workmanship. He introduced himself with a name not uncommon to the country but in his presence it was very obvious he was no ordinary man. There was something about his demeanor, the light from his eyes, or the lilt of his head. He told me there was something important he wanted me to know and he would let me share completely in a wondrous gift, one that I'd already begun to receive. I believed him. Were he a madman I thought, he might have already killed me while in the throes of my dream and I could not have resisted though I should see no purpose that he might do so.

He asked that I swear a vow of secrecy. How could I refuse? He held me completely in awe as he related that he'd been a shepherd like me until recently when having chanced upon this very cave he was attacked by a brutish animal resembling a man but possessing certain features of an animal, possibly a dog and that he'd been forced to kill the thing. He'd done it with the broad staff he carried which he'd narrowed to a point at one end used in order to test for fertility of the ground as he traveled. The beast had managed to bite him though, his wound being so severe as to prevent him traveling from the cave for many days. He only survived from eating of the flesh and blood of his attacker. He said he experienced the same transformation he'd just witnessed

16

in me and to make it complete, I must share in his flesh and blood as well. Even though I somehow knew he'd already shared my blood I obliged him by doing what he asked, consuming a small quantity of his offered blood. I felt an immediate change even more dramatic now and knew that I was in some way godlike, like him. He had chosen me he said and I felt honored to even be in his presence. And I could now be a disciple if I wished to tell others of the gift he'd been telling me of while I slept. I found it fascinating. He also mentioned that he'd learned of my own life in a like fashion and was impressed with my knowledge of carpentry, a field that interested him as well. There weren't a lot of vocation options in those days as you can well imagine. I decided against the discipleship however, I'm not as outgoing as he may have hoped. And wonderful feelings aside, whatever he had planned was sure to prove a difficult road, if not insurmountable. But I left feeling renewed, thankful and not just the least godly. And I did retain his vow of secrecy some two thousand years regarding his own transformation. No mean feat I should add, but this year people the world over celebrate the second millennial anniversary of his birth so I decided to... say something at least of him.

He was a truly remarkable man, magician, wise man, god... Call him what you will he had the best understanding of the gift and put it to the best use of any I have known. I met him only once again after our meeting in the cave. It was a habit in that time of crucifixions for vampires to be among the mourners as human blood was usually readily available. I'd heard they'd crucified the king of the Jews and knew it must be him. I saw he'd been nailed to a huge cross, without strength enough to help himself. He'd faced the sun... three times, and still it had taken a long time for him to die.

I Spend My Daze in Conversation

Many times late at night I go quietly out of my mind. The boredom, the routines of stalking the unwitting victims, the endless stream of ennui that flows through the night like water through a filthy gutter... Sometimes it's hard to find intelligent life, or just decent companionship to get you through the night. And when I'm feeling particularly crazy, when a night of spitting on cats, leering at young girl's breasts and acts of vampirism are not nearly enough to mollify me, I head over to a bar I know on the south side called The Rafters.

The people that hang there aren't people in the usual sense, not to say they're all vampires but most are what you might call vampire groupies though they may not realize it. The first thing to strike you about the place of course is the hours. It doesn't open till midnight and then it may close in an hour or not until dawn depending, which I'll explain in a minute or two. There aren't big crowds, never in fact, but the customers that come are as loyal as dogs. Some are rich playboys, others long shore construction types, a few ex-cons and some who just try to look invisible in long coats. Their perversions run the gamut from mild interest and tacit approval about what goes on to utter fascination and insane revelry. And some like to scream out their lungs within the confines of the club's padded walls. This can considerably boost the excitement level for all concerned. Naturally when girls are there they do most of the screaming, but it doesn't matter really because the place is very well

19

insulated as I've said, soundproofed really, and quite secret.

And also as I said before the customers are loyal. They have to be because the owner happens to be a vampire. He'll know if someone's been talking to the wrong people about things. That's naughty and he'll find out, then there'll be no more Santa Claus for them. And all the regular patrons know that yes Virginia, there most definitely is a Santa Claus! Though catering to the whims of vampires and miscreants can be a tall order, it's pretty obvious that no one wants to spoil it. Where else could they go to realize or at least witness their deepest perversions?

You're probably thinking I'm crazy but to me, a vampire, these people are more real and I can relate to them. And perversion is in the eye of the beholder I always say! The owner, Klaus he calls himself, pronouncing it with a German accent, probably runs a risk letting vampires in or catering to them actually... being a difficult lot to control. But he's known me for years, and most would never cause trouble for another vampire. Ethics have a place, albeit a small place, in our lives after all.

I like to go down there because even if there's nothing happening and it might close early at least there are a bunch of crazy people anticipating something crazy and that tends to help make for interesting conversation. Klaus rarely disappoints however. He is a very formidable vampire with a real gift. Call it what you may... hypnosis, mind control, seduction. And simply put, he has an insatiable appetite for the female sex far and above what would be considered normal blood requirements... For by midnight each night he finds the most alluring captivating young girls imaginable, sometimes several and often mere sexual adolescents. He might be dealt with harshly by most were he a human but as if he were some movie or rock star he holds their frail wills in his hands as so much straw. Besides what they might remember later is only a highly charged sexual dream at best. You might call it a catch and release program, same as in fishing only with him it's like fishing in the proverbial barrel, no contest. He is a master pure and simple, while many vampires struggle for a moment's opportunity to feed he is the gourmet, a true Don Juan able to relish every conquest as if at his complete leisure.

And he is generous to a fault. Once I'd gone to The Rafters hoping to drink heavily from the neck of some drugged or drunken sod because I'd been so depressed for weeks I could hardly feed myself. The reason of course, a romance... I'd been completely taken by the infectious beauty and charm of a pretty young girl who flirted so openly, so lovingly that it had been I who had been hypnotized. I felt the fool, completely useless. I'd left her there where I'd found her, some beach wares shop or sun cream store I think it was... but returned often looking for another chance. I lost hope of seeing her again until Klaus entered the club with her on his arm one night. He introduced her and realizing we'd met insisted I participate in the night's entertainment. I drooled at the prospect. When she looked at me her eyes showed a glimmer of recognition, hope and affection. While when she looked at Klaus it was plain to see fear mixed with excitement, and also resignation for the imminent sexual encounters to follow.

It was a dream. He made love to her masterfully. She was wild and untamed making it appear a rape yet submitting enough for a satisfying result. Then it was my turn, we wrestled a short time and as if on cue she melted into a simmering kettle of something like love I suppose. And though it seemed to me to last only an instant before it was over, to those present still priceless entertainment I'd wager...

As reward for a show tantamount to perfection she was allowed to leave soon afterward and I followed cornering her against a large plate glass window of an abandoned store. I held her, we kissed and talked about crazy things, improper and important things, but not anything I would remember well later. She had hypnotized me again I guess.

I followed her home and was glad to know where I could find her again even if she were doomed to forget. In all the excitement I realized I'd been too dazed to remember to even drink. Well I was sure at least Klaus, realizing my infatuation, had not imbibed to overindulgence. No matter, I would ask her if she might like to go out tomorrow night. I was sure she'd say yes. And if she didn't I could always tell Klaus about where to find her if he didn't already know... Madness has its rewards after all, and no lunatic in his wrong mind would consider denying them.

Whilst You Will, Whither You Won't

"Would you want to know me if you had the chance? Would you choose immortality if it meant a change, even a small change in your humanity?" The preacher implored. The emphasis on the word 'humanity' was just a little more than she could bear.

She switched the set off with a look of disgust. The question, she thought was when these evangelists would change. They were all bad but probably the ones on TV the worst, she decided. After all they could reach the most people, do the most harm with greatest effect.

She slipped the tight sweater along her arms and the over her head. She loved the feel of the imitation cashmere or whatever it was against her sensitive skin. Did salvation really depend on how well a televangelist could deliver a smooth line? She wondered. God she was bored. Everything she heard these days seemed to be a pickup line from men and women alike, yet nothing turned her on. Maybe she was dead inside, maybe she did need salvation. She would make sure it did not come from the likes of Grant Jackson in his yellow tux and his shining church of the glitterati... What goes with cashmere? She couldn't think. Suede hip hugging ultra shorts, she'd seen something similar in a fashion mag last week. Why not... She had a ready quip from an article titled, 'Beating off your Fashion Beasts,' at least if she ran into some hag or bozo that wanted to give her the third degree.

She thought she'd try a visit to the museum, should be a much lower ratio of creeps. She hadn't been in quite awhile, she might even learn something about art. She didn't know why she hated them all, the boyfriends, coworkers, acquaintances or the weirdos that came up to her in the street. Well she knew why she hated the weirdos who attempted to latch onto her without so much as a passing word of introduction. They either couldn't help themselves or realized they would only be giving her warning if they feigned politeness or normalcy, and would never get close enough to get that all important feel. Life in the city equals the presence of weirdos, there was no way around it. But the others worried her. A lot of the men she knew had genuine feelings for her but she just couldn't make time for them. She couldn't help that she hurt their feelings but she wasn't playing hard to get. She needed affection too but being obviously attractive somehow just didn't add up to happiness. Maybe she was the freak, emotionally or whatever! The thought made her shiver as she parked her car and hurried along the windy sidewalk toward the museum's steps.

She tried to imagine what the big picture of her life might look like. There were so many minor upsets and depressions it would definitely be in the morbid or morose genre... maybe like Edvard Munch's painting of 'The Scream.' Hopefully not that bad. She remembered hearing the news of that painting's theft... in broad daylight by armed gunmen. The curator had been concerned about the fine line between security and allowing museum patrons to view the art unhindered. Unhindered, that was what she wanted to be too.

She walked along the marble floors and was thankful for the recessed alcoves that tended to isolate the observer from the mainstream walking traffic. There were ceiling cameras everywhere. She wondered how that must frustrate the weirdos. Then again maybe they had an opposite effect, lulling the victim into secure complacency while the molester delivered his feel with a masterful coup de grace! She'd be ready in any case. The cases usually gave themselves away mixing plaids and stripes, wrong socks, cliché trench coats, or something stupid.

She gazed at the large mélange of dark blues and browns, and noted the rough surface texture of 'oil paint on canvas,' apparently the title and even a price tag to boot. The artist was still alive then. What would it be like to meet an actual artist? Not this one, she thought. The title was really lacking. She moved on before the familiar 'let down' mode could take hold.

A few sculptures decorated the main walkway. She supposed they were only cast copies as anyone might accidentally bump one. Or more likely she'd be knocked into one herself by an enterprising weirdo. She only paused long enough for a glance then on to more paintings. There were beautiful prints and special glass enclosed photographs and many more paintings. It seemed sad that most of the real paintings were so bizarre, not of definable entities but just colors. Maybe they were period works, something like modern impressionist pseudo-neo-classic but with obvious Paleolithic influences. She laughed at the idea then checked to see that no one was too close to be bothered. On the street she'd known her laugh to attract a flock of weirdos. Things remained tranquil, she relaxed.

There were a few works that affected her, that drew her in, that made her want to reach out to touch or consider them closely. The prices seemed high on those though. She finally came to the larger rooms in the back and then an entrance to a smaller room that was darkened allowing the paintings to be lit by muted colorful lights. The room was empty except for a single tall man in an attractive coat. His coat and features were dark and she almost missed seeing him at all but there he stood toward the back staring fixedly at one of the paintings. She admired the paintings casually until she found herself at the man's side. He turned to her nonchalantly and smiled. She was immediately struck by the charming manner in which he looked at her. "Interesting motif, would you agree?" She ventured. He nodded and looked back to his painting.

"You seem fascinated by that one, you didn't do it yourself did you?" She asked. He smiled but still wouldn't talk. She decided to try at least once more. How awkward she mused, how often had she met someone who'd barely acknowledge her, maybe the poor lighting... "Well I just couldn't help notice you seem an attractive man but I can't tell your age. You dress older but your face seems so young. Excuse me for asking... are you wearing makeup?" He looked her way again but remained silent. "I mean it's probably okay if you do. I do some modeling work myself. You seem to have the look the agencies go for, you know," she stammered, "pale, tall, kind of rugged..."

He gazed intently into her eyes a moment and said, "let me love you." Simply and just like that she thought in the brief instant that followed, "Isn't that just my luck?" Still it wasn't so much what he said but the way and the melodic sound of his voice. She could almost give it consideration... During her hesitation she closed her eyes just a second and immediately felt a comfortable warmth at her throat. His loving embrace surrounded her sending her senses reeling. But when she opened her eyes he was gone. She touched the warm moist feeling at her neck and found blood on her fingertips though he'd been so gentle.

"That's really something," she thought. "A guy like that being a big sicko. It just doesn't figure. Well that does it, I think I'll settle for anything now... an evangelist, scientologist, a psychiatrist maybe, hell even a pathologist! Why not?"

The Scarlet Battalion

Stories of *war* could fascinate the men of this small town, as they do the men from most small Midwest towns. The women were another matter entirely, but when there was someone talking war it was always from a time before women were allowed in the military. What the females might be doing or saying during a story then was roundly ignored.

Of course not all the men were great with a story but most had seen action of some kind and not a few had spent years fighting Germans, Koreans or the Vietnamese and were relentless talkers. Sometimes this necessitated changing some facts to fit the flow of the story or adding details that may have been forgotten or dropped in favor of increasing the entertainment value. Most men frowned on this practice but if it came down to deciding a tale's relative merit or not hearing it at all there was no contest.

The best audience might usually be found in a tavern, the benches at the Post Office and park, or the barber shop on Fridays. If several potential tellers were gathered, the topic of war might be broached in some subtle way such as,

"Who was it shooting last night, sounded like a .45?"

Another'd add, "No, more likely a rifle, say probably 1500 foot per second muzzle."

"Heck it was me," d'say a third. "Just testing that mail-order assault rifle I got myself last Christmas, only blanks though..." Then a few minutes later they'd jump in with a grizzly tale of murderous mayhem complete with all the expletives from A to Z, or sometimes with code words for the obscenities as everything had to be coded for routine communications in war. It was just habit after a short while and now tended to add to the realism of a really great story as well as helping distract and irritate any women present.

Usually those with the lowest rank might start with standard horrors or atrocities until catching the interests of a retired officer who'd then rattle on about this offensive or that complete with alternate strategies, counter attacks, propaganda, statistics, and the battle's effect on the war itself. Sometimes men would just listen and no one 'be sure if they had been in war themselves or not, because they might be too old to do much talking or for some personal reason, etc. would rarely participate actively. One of these older guys was named Chief, and not much was known of him because he kept company with the oldest men of the town who were mostly regarded as senile or worse, crazy.

Once during a story session the teller said something to cause Chief to say a few unintelligible words and he was hushed to silence though he'd been ambling away from the group at the time. After he'd gone they'd say, "Don't listen to him that old coot's crazy as a loon!"

Then the other, "Maybe. What's a coot anyway?"

"I don't know, some kind of loon..." And they'd start another story.

One day out of the blue when they all just happened to be gathered at the tavern but for some strange reason no stories were being told old Chief slammed a fist on the bar and shouted, "You punk's don't know notthin about war!" The men looked with wide eyes at first thinking he must be crazy until they realized it was the first time anyone had heard him speak clearly... "I served with the Scarlet Battalion, the fiercest regimen, er uh company any army's ever seen from any time up until just about now!"

One of the officers spoke up, "Chief, you got a story for us, go-ahead. Ours were just about to turn boring one of these years. First tell us what war though, not the Civil I hope!" He laughed as did the others quite heartily.

The old man stared at nothing in particular and paused for a moment then said, "It was the Civil, you tart!" Then shouting, "And where's my drink then?"

The bartender looked up shocked, "Well what do want? I don't know any colonial drinks!" They laughed again, even louder... The old man just waved him away as if he really didn't want anything anyway.

"Well," Chief continued, "I can tell you a story to make you pass out, puke and leave your wives, or forget about leaving your wives, whatever's worse!" The laughter subsided slowly and someone yelled, "Tell us about the scarlet battalion, puking doesn't bother me and I'd enjoy the other things you said!"

"All right then," Chief replied. "We was basically a bunch of vampires that didn't like the way the war was going and wanted to help the Union. Of course we could do things on our own but we wanted to form a group that could link up to a high-level command with privy to what all was really happening, intelligence and all that..."

"Vampires?" One of the older officers said in a high voice. "There's no such thing and you'd be younger even so. What army would enlist an old codger saying he's a vampire?"

"A good point but I was younger then and I only aged some because I don't follow the rules too good. A vampire's got to do this and that, and can't do this and that. It's a damned pain in the neck... but you're right. Them damned officers didn't want to have nothing to do with us. Thought we was crazy and locked us up right away. Of course the next day we wasn't there and that set them thinking some. Well they thought we were even more crazy when we arrived the next evening with the same request. See it's an act of treason to go against orders even if those orders were for you to be locked up. So some of the officers wanted us shot right way but Grant, he said no. That's right

29

General Grant himself, we went to where we knew he was camped because there was no avoiding that our appearances and coming forward the way we did would cause problems... but we thought, and rightly so, that the only way we'd be provided war information was to announce who we were and what we could do... that second bit would take some doing however because they still decided we should be locked up and so we were. But at least they didn't shoot us right then!"

"I'll wait till the finish to decide whether or not you've gone off your warm milk and crackers or whatever it is a man, excuse me, vampire your age should eat," a young officer interrupted. "But let me just ask why vampires would bother about war or care which side won?"

"Good question, I was just about getting to that, you young trout! You see that's what they called green recruits back then as they smelled strong of fear you know... The way most of 'em were made us want to turn 'em all vampire you know, to save their lives. Cause they'd get themselves killed faster somehow, I don't know why. Maybe they gave 'em names like that so that those left could have more confidence, you know... more likely, the trouts got killed cause they didn't run, you know retreat, when it came time or they ran too soon so were shot by their own officers sad to say."

"But what us vampires wanted most was just an end to the war because it really was an all-out war. You didn't know if your cemetery or house what have you would be there from night to night. Mansions were routinely commandeered, larders raided, root cellars turned upside down, servants taken from more important work... We knew the Union had more men, better supplies. Lincoln himself looked like a vampire and he wanted to help the slaves. If he helped slaves maybe he'd want to free vampires as well... maybe we'd be accepted, free to walk openly with people knowing who we were and without fear. A lot of us don't prefer secrecy really and have no intentions to kill... That part of it may have been a far fetched dream. Who knows though, the man been killed too soon. And there had been a plan to vampirize him, Lincoln of course, about the time he'd been killed, so things might have been very different. To make things worse... it'd been rumored also we was involved though we weren't, and that there was some informant vampire carrying news to political circles. So that may be the reason vampires tend to remain solitary creatures to this day since the scarlet battalion..."

"Well what was it exactly that these red Devils did do if I may call them that?" Asked an officer to some renewed laughing.

"If you listen I'll say. You remember we'd been arrested and thrown in irons again. This time leg irons and a double guard. Of course though we numbered more than sixty we easily made our escape. We learned one important detail from Grant's camp and that was that an important battle was to be fought for Richmond and if Grant could make it there first with his armies the war might well be won. We immediately flew with haste to Lee's encampment bringing the only uniforms available, those from killed Union soldiers. Then we proceeded to parade in a fashion, which was probably not too correct since that sort of thing was typically practiced by day. But we used our imaginations, and were sufficiently convincing as we marched through a field very near Lee's headquarters, so that we were ordered fired upon. We were close enough to be seen by moonlight and sentry fires but were not overtaken for fear of ambush, especially since it was apparent that we were not bothering to return fire ourselves. It was reported by scouts though that our uniforms contained gaping hole's and were drenched in blood and that we continued to march. Several hundred men, confederate soldiers, probably hardened veterans fired on us for an hour I'd say but not one of us fell. In the morning just before dawn we vanished into the morning mist as vampires do, leaving the uniforms behind and Lee himself looked on as he drank his morning coffee. The result was that they did delay, additional scouting missions were ordered and the incident carefully considered, although somehow never recorded..."

31

After a long while the bartender finally spoke up, "Were you wounded old man?"

"Forty nine times, now there's your war story!" Chief said pointing at the man and nodding before walking slowly outside to join other old men waiting there. When he reached the door he paused, "'Course I been shot lots more 'an that since... but not recently. Might kill me now if any of you were thinkin to put my story to a test!" He laughed.

None Remains Save One

"So what do you think? Is this the most vainglorious job there is or what?" "I don't know what you're talking about. What's glorious in cleaning grime off centuries old stone?   I'm covered in filth! It was vain of you to insist on my help I guess!"

"You just got to have vision. Someday you'll see. You'll be on your knees thanking me. Hell you should already! What other scientist, archaeologist, historian, grave digger would be allowed near Castle Dracula with free reign and a commission from the Hungarian Historical Preservation Society?"

"Well we don't have free reign. We have a license to clean and that's it. Any findings have got to be reported for their decision. I've got to admit I don't know how you did it, you're really not any of those things. You take one course of anthropology at Cambridge and you'd think you'd won the Nobel Prize."

"Well you're a scientist and I've got killer references." "I don't doubt it with your ability to talk. It is a change of pace anyway and I'm grateful at least for that John. I thought this castle was already completely restored and commercialized for the tourist trade. I'd been on the tour myself and it was an interesting presentation but the original building design is obviously quite simple."

"You see doctor, that's where you're wrong, and why even with your degrees you're still a bit of an understudy. Because a good enthusiast would know the castle consisted of more than what's been restored for the tour!"

"Sure I remember reading about the basement were Dracula supposedly had his spare emergency caskets and the treasure room and his private locker room high in the parapet of sorts. All of it just commercial propaganda and hearsay..."

"Naturally you wouldn't expect that treasure still be lying about and it said right in the book he had fifty caskets of earth sent to London after he'd given Jonathan Harker his errands, remember?"

"Sure, sure... the book, 'Dracula' you mean?"

"And that room high in the tower was just a lookout so Harker 'not know his real bedroom!"

"Paranoid sort no doubt. I'm glad at least the society didn't fabricate a royal vampire bedchamber complete with coffin centerpiece just to dupe any gullible tourists."

"That probably isn't it. The main thing is accessibility. If this damn country weren't so inhospitable then there might be more tourists. As it is they'd just be wasting money on some elaborate recreation."

"John, you know your realism is almost refreshing, almost!"

"Hey what's this Doc? Notice how the color of the mortar in this section is slightly darker than the rest after cleaning, and the stones too seem to be of different origin?"

"Your right, that whole section of wall may have been added later. This room doesn't seem to make much sense does it, maybe there's treasure?"

"It'd be nice wouldn't it, Doc? That's why I wanted to start back here. Look it's a small room, what... about ten by ten near ground level with no apparent function and not even an entrance, just a small window. It's located at the back of the castle which we know extends into the mountain, the most protected area. I estimate that the wall separating us from the main dining hall is six feet plus. Whoever constructed it didn't want it part of any tour!"

"You may well be right John, but I suppose we'd better report the news before going ahead."

"I'm thinking we really don't have a report until we take a bit more of a look. Besides how'd you like to go make some vague report and be replaced by someone who'd make some fantastic discovery in your place?"

"Well it's your call. I'm just the understudy..."

"Right, here goes... That old mortar doesn't stand up well against modern sledge hammer and muscle does it?"

"I'd say, but look it's only another wall and nothing else. It looks to be of a similar style as the rest and apparently wasn't needed for repair of any kind."

"Wait now, there are a few more blocks here at the base. What's that some writing? Yes definitely writing!"

"An inscription in stone, translating to 'None Remains, Save One!' Interesting at least."

"Very. And nice work but not of restoration quality. That's been here hundreds of years."

"No question. But what could it mean?"

"I know Doc, a siege! The castle was overrun and only one vampire remained to be entombed before he could be captured."

"Well it couldn't have been Dracula, your holy book states pretty clearly what became of him! Maybe you should check your concordance for the phrase, 'None Remains, Save One' before we proceed?"

"Sounds kind of like a joke doesn't it? ' None Remains,' but 'Save One' anyway? Or how about this, it could be a riddle. It's got the words 'Remains' and 'Save'... Take away the 'None' and 'One', switch 'em around and it's 'Save Remains!' Vampire humor!"

"Not bad for a five hundred year old joke, John. If I remember the Castle's history, it's more likely that massacres occurring here were at Dracula's hand and utilized all manner of torture such as nailing guest's hats to their heads, and impaling them feet first on huge vertical greased poles..."

"Of course, he once invited the entire town to the castle on a pretense of compromise over some dispute. Then after the banquet had them all impaled, if the legends are true."

"Exactly! But I think the phrase must be some reference to vampires since it was owned by one..."

"Right, well maybe early in its building the castle was overrun as you said and maybe Dracula was away at war, which according to legend he often was as a young man. Suppose someone else had charge of the castle, say his father... And he had this constructed some time before he was killed. The historical record is incomplete regarding the father, Dracul the Dragon as he was known. Then the phrase might make sense if workers out of honor to his memory had his tomb inscribed."

"You've got it or maybe he directed the inscription himself with a dying request to signify his son. Look below the inscription near the floor... something else. Let me clear away the dirt."

"A dragon carved into the stone John. It must be!"

"And look Doc near the sides of the slab are impressions. Let me clean them up. Yeah and handles. I bet we can slide this head stone or whatever it is right out of the wall."

"All right then, let's go on three. One, two... it moved!"

"Just a little more... Do you see it? Here with the flashlight, an absolutely fabulous coffin, Doc!"

"I don't suppose I'd be able to talk you into returning to the historical society for a thorough discussion first?"

"Not likely, and that's what it is, just a small burial chamber big enough for a big fashionable coffin of stone. Must have been top-of-the-line for its day... We can't remove it. We're going to have to crawl in the crypt and take a look!"

"Sure why not just crawl into the previously undiscovered crypt of Dracula's father. That doesn't sound too scary. If it's not too cliché what time is it? I left my watch in my case..."

"Well go-ahead scramble in, I think we both can fit. Look, there at the end of the coffin, a fine sword and shield with the Dragon's crest. Treasure after all! Ready, let's slide the lid on three. One, two... Oh my God!"

"Doc, open your eyes. Don't faint, there's nothing here it was just the noise from the lid!"

"There is something John, right in the middle there... ash."

"Right doc, a small pile of ash... shine the light. See, there something else in it. Sure enough, a ring! Huh, achoooh! Excuse me."

"God bless you, c'mon let's go!"

"Wait Doc, oh okay I can't see anything with this dust anyway. Look at this baby Doc... here I'll put it on."

"Wait!"

"What? Too late."

"That wasn't dust you know, suppose..."

"Yeah it was that ash. It's like powder when you sneeze on it."

"Did you breathe it John?"

"Well yeah, I had to. But take a look at this. Imagine being able to say you've worn the ring of Dracul, the Dragon!"

"But don't you recall stories of vampire ash being re-animated by contact with human blood?"

"Yes go on... Jeez, you didn't cut your hands did you Doc?"

"No, your lungs John. The only organ of the body where the capillaries, containing a network of miles of microscopic blood vessels are practically in direct contact with the air. In fact just a single cell layer of lung alveoli and capillary endothelium keep the blood from direct contact with the air!"

"English, Doc please!"

"Lung cells have spaces between them, pores for the diffusion of gases from blood to air and... air to blood!"

"I bet you used to be a smoker didn't you Doc? You know I do a feel a bit different, do you mind turning off the flashlight... or at least not shining it in my eyes?"

"John, look at your teeth!"

"What's the matter Doc? I'm not scaring you am I? Doc? Fainting will only make things... easier!"

Cute But Functional

She had the kind of hair that smelled like summer rain, her eyes sparkled like fine champagne, but she wasn't happy. She didn't want to hate of course. It was just the people around her, the situations she found herself in... circumstances which turned out to be just about her entire life. High school had been somewhat okay, the loathing hadn't really started until after school, though there had been heavy periods of weirdness in college before she discovered the cause.... or at least what seemed to be the cause at the time.

She knew she was attractive, the admiring glances told her as much and she was pleasant to be around. At least she didn't try to put anybody off, if a guy wanted to talk she'd smile and listen. She may not say much but she was never blatantly bitchy. Did some guys actually like that, a girl to be mean to them so they could be mean right back? Sure someone acts mean to be cool, as a joke or out of the thoughtlessness and the wrong person's listening. He can't understand and it gets into his head he's been abused for no reason so now it's his turn to do the abusing. Once the cycle of sick abuse starts it gains momentum until someone decides it's not cool or funny or grows a brain. That's not fair. Just because a girl might be a little thoughtless was no reason for, whatever! What was it? She couldn't even name it. She knew only she didn't like it, she hated it.

The things they'd say, acquaintances, people she barely knew... 'She's cute and functional!' emphasizing the *'and.'* Or 'She's got what it takes and knows how to use it! And how!' would be the reply. And 'Show us how you take it, we wanna see ya make it!' The lines were endless and it was sexual harassment, plain and simple straight from the mean streets of New York. So why was it happening to her? Other people that heard it stood and did nothing as if they were all in on it, girls included. Or worse yet, they thought she deserved it. But what had she done? She dressed conservatively, nice clothes yes but she didn't flaunt anything.

Once in school she thought it might have started as a bad locker room joke. Some jock made up a sexy story about her to look big. That time she walked past a group of guys standing in the hall near the gym looking athletic and heard them laughing like she were some joke and one guy looking at her kind of embarrassed like he was trying to get her to wave... but she couldn't, it was too weird.

The worst thing was that she couldn't attract a real boyfriend who might be able to protect her from the weirdness. The last thing she wanted to do was go overboard with effort which would only make things much worse. Did she actually look that good that most guys presumed she was a hot bed of sin, literally crawling with infectious organisms? But this was a progressive area, high literacy, high-quality jobs, competitive schools. Sometimes it felt as if they meant no harm, those strangers who would talk loudly when she happened to be near.

And it wasn't always blatantly rude or sexual talk, though that was always the worst. It was almost as if someone had paid an entire town to needle her each in their private horribly twisted ways and yet they were all together, united in weirdness. Sometimes she screamed when she knew no one could hear or got drunk or lost herself in music. The good times never lasted more than a day or two and there'd be the DJ on the car radio talking about something she'd just done not an hour before, or the television news man referring to a course assignment she was currently having trouble with. Of course it all seemed a bit like the Pleasantville movie that had starred Jim Carrey but differed in a major way. Instead of being a public star of her own private life, she was also hated and vilified in the role. The jives though subtle and indirect possessed invisible accuracy, painful accuracy... Perhaps this was what happened to Howard Hughes?

She was a kind of invisible celebrity but why? Celebrities only had a few of their moments categorized although the tabloids tended to attack at the worst times, she seemed to be under a constant barrage. What celebrity would stand for that? And she wasn't even one. She wondered sometimes how things might change if she were to actually become a star, ten times worse, a hundred times worse? Could there even be the remote possibility of that? She guessed that probably everyone at one time or other harbored those bizarre desires. If those types of dreams were even slightly similar to what she was enduring she would have no part of it. She thought to try modeling in hopes that maybe that would calm the demons. If the demons were trying to obscenely direct her life in some way maybe modeling was an answer. She went to the studios with some of her best pix, slang for pictures in the business, but they never called. Good she thought, she didn't really want that anyway. She'd be on file if some demon movie producer thought he could use her otherwise she didn't need the anxiety.

Eventually she tried changing her appearance, trying to be fat, dyeing her hair and bad haircuts. Sunglasses, odd clothes, a pet cat, a new apartment, then a new town... Nothing changed but the names and faces, and the longer she remained the more it became her nightmare. If she were maimed, sick or dying, how would they like it then she wondered? At least she felt that her parents cared for her, and she certainly didn't want to introduce any radical issues that might alter that such as *'paranoid delusions of persecution.'*

She couldn't give up, it especially helped at times as she discovered the mischief was not always malevolent although when you saw seven-year old kids tossing beer bottles on your yard it only makes you remember when the twelve year-olds broke them in the road the week before. When you hear car horns or loud trucks just minutes before your wake-up clock goes off every day, and when the demons know what you like to eat, how often you think of sex, what your favorite color is... it makes you think how severe the taunting can be especially when you're checking account is low, or an important call forgotten, or date missed. Maybe she did think of *it* too often... but what was that to them?

Some of her friends remained somewhat loyal in these difficult times, friends she made at the start of high school or before. Others had changed with time, or due to the weirdness or both. What worried her most was that it would get to her eventually, this abusive weirdness and she'd become just as 'evil' or whatever the weirdness represented. She was intimate with evils' familiar tug at her sleeve. She had a feeling there would be no repercussions in resorting to it on occasion when she'd been sorely tempted. She'd resisted, and instead pointed out abusers, threatened to inform on them or actually did call police at times only to realize that the police themselves were part of it... She could hardly bring herself to say it, the '*conspiracy.*' That was the word *they* used as the hallmark of the deranged psycho mind!

Her employment was little different from her private life except that the weirdness was if anything more intense. It tended to have fluctuations or come in waves though and if she willed herself through the first few months of a new job then the threats of imminent termination lessened.

She often asked herself, 'Was she being taught or somehow guided to a supernatural purpose?' If so when would it manifest? At this point she might consider an appointment to a position as 'supergirl' acceptable. She'd really be able to give the weirdos a workout with superpowers! Or maybe she could be a stand up comic, comedy most times seemed her only refuge. She was surprised anxiety hadn't already put her in the hospital, a victim of stress induced heart attack. Then the doctors could turn into ogres and torment her and say there's nothing wrong... and laugh.

Sometimes it seemed as if God himself had something in store for her. She thought about the boy from high school who had called her, 'cute and functional' all those years ago. It still sounded obscene. How would he know? And if she *was* so cute and functional why hadn't he tried to get her into bed? And why hadn't any of the others to whom she'd given the signals much like a quarterback in a superbowl game, unmistakable signals... only to be benched? Why hadn't they wanted to play? Maybe they just didn't want to play nice.

On the day following her 26th birthday she woke realizing she'd overslept. She'd done a little drinking but now it was already dusk. She noticed a note on her dresser that read, 'My Darling, I hope you're not upset I haven't been by to see you since that night, ten years ago. You were sixteen and attending your prom. You were far too beautiful to be left on your own... I never let your date touch you, remember? I've been keeping tabs ever since. I vowed to protect and never forget. To me you were my 'little star.' Last night you received your inheritance. I hope it serves you well... Your Vampire Dad, D.

She felt her neck and looked in the mirror to see to puncture marks together at one side just as her reflection began to fade.

'Oh a vampire,' she thought. 'That seemed right somehow didn't it? And she'd hoped things wouldn't get worse...'

'Some father, she didn't even know his name!'

A Sweet Young Wine, Yet Satisfying to the Palate

"Let her go, Zice, that's disgusting!"

"Hold on Zuir, almost done, mmmm." He let her loose with a loud smack of his lips and let the body drop with a limp thud. "Excellent vintage. I'd guess a '69 tossed child, with full bouquet of birth control hormones, high adrenaline and sweet erogenous sweat, you know from the breasts, neck and under arms..."

"Jeez, the keyword here is was, *was* an excellent vintage! You destroyed the vineyard. What's left for me or the others? What about later? You never think ahead Zice."

"Don't you ever follow the feeling, your instincts Zuir? We are vampires after all. Go with the flow, blood flow that is. Uh? It's good to the last drop so don't stop till it pops. Or something like that, how does that commercial go? Besides if I was 'kind to every living creature' like your Casper vampire friends we'd be up to our necks in vampires. Then naturally some would want revenge and start killing us all. Remember that one that cut off your..."

"I'm not telling you to make babies just show a little discretion, and not be so gluttonous. She could have lasted weeks!"

"I bet by the time you get to be my age Zuir you won't be saving your favorites either. Do humans share their favorite wines and girlfriends?" They are momentarily distracted by a heaving convulsion racking the dying girl's unconscious body.

"Don't you remember your favorite toy, your first bike, or that twelve scoop ice cream sundae you'd never share even when you knew you couldn't eat it all?" Zuir looked at the breathless girl beautiful in her lurid pose of death.

"No I don't remember because I'm not human anymore! We can't be human again can we so stop trying to cloud the issue with your false sentimentality!" Zuir considers the girl carefully, "Why don't you give some back maybe she'll live?"

"No, no chance of that. She's a dry wine now, one of the driest. She a port of no entry in a non-returnable bottle."

"You really are loathsome sometimes, Zice."

"It's my blood now, it'd just be wasted on her unless you wanted to take care of her. Otherwise she'd be orphaned. A vampire is a terrible thing to waste as we all know!"

"I think the phrase is... the hell with it. I never want to be as old as you! I bet you really don't know your favorites as well as you say. I mean blood's a serious topic to a vampire. I know I've been drinking ten years compared to hundreds for you but I haven't tasted anything near this good as you describe, say really exquisite..."

"See for yourself Zuir. Turn her over. What little is left will be collecting in parts nearest the floor. Take a little nip and see for yourself."

"That *is* good. It's really hormones that make the difference or probably just genetic right? Maybe some particular RH factor or hemoglobin like that sickle cell that has a special taste? Perhaps she just grew up barefoot in a French vineyard drinking wine all her life? Uh?"

"It's hard to be that scientific about an emotional topic like blood but since inquiring minds want to know I'd say it's a special combination of things, like the homemade lasagna your mother used to make. Not mine, lasagna's a little after her time. But you have your herbs such as oregano and basil, leave out the devil's claw and the wolfbane though. That's a joke, Zuir!"

"Who cares about lasagna already? I admit I used to eat it ravenously but I haven't given it a thought in ten years now! Why would a vampire bother about food?"

"Well you may do well to remember that sometimes you are what you eat. You can tell can't you when someone's been eating garlic recently, how the blood has that sharp pungent taste... some foods can have a positive effect. You'd prefer someone fresh from a gourmet restaurant over an alcoholic off the street wouldn't you? It goes without saying... so the diet determines the *noodle* quality of the lasagna which can ruin things if not cooked right. The cholesterol levels naturally would be the cheese where too much is always better than none at all. The sex hormones, the spice and herbs while the real pizazz is the epinephrine sauce. Your adrenaline may be a hormone technically but it's what's there from fear. Fear matters! Now there is a vampire bumper sticker! Better than *No Fear* anyway."

"Sure you're right Zice. It seems so morbid cause you can't help feeling sorry, you know empathy, sometimes. A civilized vampire always tries to avoid it as much as possible. Who wants to be a monster with an abnormal brain? Vampires can be sophisticated, not uncouth, a little moral if they want to be... So why not try?"

"Yes it's okay to be conservative *Caspers* milking human cows for a while then you get tired of Mr. Nice Guy... you'll see. Like celebrities need their drugs... Of course you wimps might end up buying it at the pharmacies but it's really not the same. It loses potency for vampires if it's not in the blood. Once you start experimenting you'll be hooked."

"Don't you mean torturing Zice?"

"Call me irresponsible Zuir. If you've ever seen big cats fling around their prey as if they were playing, what politicians do to political prisoners, how pimps beat their girls, the way those car salesman deal... then you have a hint."

"Well I guess I should ask what was your cruelest, er I mean most delicious attack? Probably ah something akin to Dracula himself I'd wager... a thorough staking on huge poles with the blood gushing down around you?"

"Actually no Zuir, wasting all that blood would defeat the purpose wouldn't it?"

"Well yeah I guess."

"To answer truthfully I'd probably have to say it was the first time. I was naturally nervous and unsure of myself but it was just do or die you know. It was the typical cemetery scene. And I overacted thinking to scare her into submission. I was still unaware of my powers and it worked. She screamed bloody murder at the sight of my fangs... I think she may have also recognized me because I knew her, so she thought I was a ghost or something you know because I'd already died by then of course. And then I miscalculated my overbite, practically chipped a tooth. It was wonderful but then you're only a virgin once!"

"Oh I see. Well my first time was regrettable and with a man. Just self defense really but at least I got a meal out of it... I had nightmares after for awhile though."

"Oh that's rich Zuir!" he laughs. "Nightmares, I'd almost forgotten. The art of dream invasion is a tricky subject but not without rewards... You play it right, you have a slave for life at your beck and call. A lost art really. You gotta have a lot of patience but it's not impossible if you keep at it, you'll see! Practice with a mirror! Sorry, 'nother bad joke..."

"I'm almost used to them by now, Zice."

Zice stares at Zuir allowing his eyes to quiver spasmodically, their pigments flaring red. "Try this... Repeat after me, I vant to drink your blaahddd!"

It Creeps with Pads and Claws

"Go on tell me again what you think it is. I want to hear you say it out loud this time please."

"Dear, I said it sounded like a wolf! And I thought women were supposed have acute hearing."

"No I have cute ears and earrings and that confuses you. Darling even with normal hearing I can tell that's not a wolf! In Hollywood, that's crazy. Say maybe somebody is doing a movie out here, but I still say it's more like a coyote or an alligator with that kind of hoarseness about it."

"So since you're from Florida you have to hear gators in the California hills? We're about halfway between Hollywood Hills and Malibu in desolate mountainous terrain carved out by glaciers and you're hearing alligators?"

"Well you don't see any glaciers out there either but that doesn't mean they're not trapped in the canyons or inside the mountain..."

He shakes his head, "I guess you got me there. How do any of us know?"

"Wait there it is again. There is a definite raspiness. I wonder what the neighbors think?"

"Our neighbors are all movie stars who probably either aren't home or have too much property to be close enough to hear anything. That's what you said you like about mountain living, the desolation, the utter desolation, remember?"

"Yes of course it's a scarce commodity in Hollywood. We probably have neighbors all around and just don't know it yet. You know how they like to build on stilts in inaccessible places. We ought to do some exploring, but let's wait until they catch the alligator."

"It's definitely not an alligator! Are you listening? Use your earrings! I'll concede a coyotes yes, even a cougar possibly but that's the limit. A long horned mountain sheep or wayward elk perhaps. There's no snapping or hissing is there?"

"A bull alligator can bellow louder than a bear, honey, and be very territorial sometimes. And I read once where artificial estuaries had been produced and alligators successfully introduced to California for the garment industry!"

"You read that in some fashion magazine no doubt? Well what did the article suggest to do when one is hunting the fierce California mountain alligator or vice versa?"

"Their legs are stumpy so they're not too good at long runs but they might hunker down in the scrub bushes and become pesky..."

"Hey dear, look out the window. I see something yellow way out in the distance."

"Eyes? Alligators have yellow eyes you know and big! When they're stalking on water their eyes stick out from the surface so they can see both in the air and underwater, like bifocals. That's why they *need* big eyes."

"Well look!"

"I can't tell it's too breezy."

"I think he's shutting them when that breeze dies down and uses that bush over there for cover when it comes up. See there a flash of yellow when the bush moves!"

"Maybe, it's too far to see really. They might be just slits since he's out of water."

"You don't say? That'd make a great picture wouldn't it? I can see the headlines, '*rare California MOUNTAIN alligator found foraging at night by vigilant Hollywood residents.*' I should be able to get close enough for a flash shot.

"You're not going out there. What about *the call?*"

"I think your right dear, that last time sounded more like a bellow than a howl. Seriously who cares about a pesky coyote? I'll just scare him off."

"Wait!"

"That's right officer, those were his last words... he was gone just a few minutes and probably got fifty yards. There's just a few scrub bushes for something to hide and not much else. Then all of a sudden I heard him yell, '*Oh my God I was...*' then nothing but gargling."

"You mean gurgling ma'am?"

"Yes I suppose that's it. He was probably trying to say I was right and he was... wrong."

"And what was he wrong about ma'am?"

"The wolf of course, weren't you listening?"

"Sorry ma'am, you say you actually saw a wolf?"

"No. My husband heard one and then later I guess he *saw* it. That's why he said, 'Oh my God *I* was *blah blah blah*.' Get it, he was wrong because he didn't see what he thought he saw! He *thought* it was just a coyote. But he wouldn't be *killed* by a coyote would he?"

"And you thought it was a crocodile?" She stares at him fiercely. "No need to get testy ma'am."

"What do you mean, 'no need to to get testy.' This is a murder isn't it?"

"We're not quite sure yet."

"What do you mean?"

"It seems your husband may have died of fright. There are no external markings, though there may have been loss of blood, were not sure yet. He was *extremely* white."

51

"Oh."

"Ma'am why would he have been outside if he expected to encounter a wolf?"

"No he didn't expect it, I mean I didn't. I thought its call was more like a bull gator. He didn't believe it but then he did and he went for a picture. See that's why he had the camera..."

"Yes we have the broken camera. When we develop the film maybe we'll have our picture of the... the alligator, (he coughs), excuse me. Ma'am did you see an *alligator*?"

"No, or a wolf or coyote or sheep... nothing. He said it had big gold eyes. I didn't see them really."

"I see." He said making notation is in his field report pad, 'big gold eyes.'

"Yes, like an alligator."

"A little respect please, if you don't mind ma'am."

"I'm telling the truth, can't you track it or something?"

"Yes, our canine team has already been over the site. Some sort of scent trail was uncovered that appeared to lead nowhere unfortunately. Tracks were seen similar to a dog's but larger, possibly a large dog or cat creature..."

"You mean a cougar or coyote then?"

"No."

"No? Then what?"

"The claws appeared very elongated."

"So you're saying alligator?"

"Ma'am I really don't know, we'll have to wait for the report." The policeman turns to leave...

"So it has paws and claws. You sure it wasn't a bear?"

"I'm afraid I don't know, ma'am. We just don't know at this point. The dog will need to get in the house however and give it a thorough going over. You don't mind?"

"No I suppose not, it's not a wolf hound or anything?"

"A bloodhound shepherd mix I think ma'am."

"That sounds unusual, well thank you detective."

"Likewise ma'am, and try not to worry. We'll be posting a man."

"Right." She said squinting into the early morning sun.

The bizarre deaths continued that summer for Los Angeles and the surrounding areas. No pictures, in the 'mountain alligator case' as it came to be known in the tabloids (naturally standard press wires refused to touch it), produced evidence. Nor did any eyewitness accounts prove fruitful in catching the elusive beast. Tracks consisting of paw pads and claws appeared and disappeared as if into thin air. There was apparently no rearing on haunches and digging in of claws to signify a lunge at the victims. It was as if the creature had been airlifted by plane, bird or magic. Perhaps even giant bat for the express purpose of... dare I say, fear at a glance?

Sing Me a Lullaby Or...

"Sing me a lullaby," he thought as he drank from the young woman's soft throat.

"What, I can't hear you," she said hoarsely while trying to deal with the enveloping awesome presence of this man or creature, whatever it was.

"I'm not talking, listen with your mind."

She concentrated. This time again she heard or rather sensed his request. "I can't," she said. "I can hardly breathe. I feel paralyzed."

"Just a lullaby or two, whispered will nicely do..." he thought.

"Am I dying?" She asked to his mind. "Why are you torturing me? What have I done to you?"

He forced himself to refrain from feeding a moment and walked with her, his huge black wings camouflaged by the shadows and appearing much like a large cape. She found herself propelled along helplessly, her feet taking rapid small steps all on their own.

"Why you were at that park bench weren't you... waiting, hoping for someone to come sweep you away, far away from the worries of today, tomorrow as well, hell! Now sing..."

"Hush little baby don't you cry, Momma's gonna sing you..."

"Not that one... too trite. Something different, new."

"Oh way down south in the land of cotton, good times there are not forgotten!"

"I haven't heard that in a while but overdone. The King did it masterfully of course but you may have guessed I'm not your typical music fan." His great wings flap lightly along her back sending an odd chill racing along her spine and raising hairs on her tingling flesh. They were off the path now and about to enter the clearing where the moon shown brightly down illuminating the grass and nocturnal insects crawling among blades. She stood transfixed with its beauty and at his hypnotic powers.

"Sometimes I hear a song once or twice and it grows tiresome. I can hardly stand it unless there is a new lovely throat to give it voice, then yes, it seems to live. Sing."

"But I'm not a singer," she thought.

"Remember!" She realized he was talking in her mind again explaining she needn't actually vocalize.

"If you know the words, you can hum the tune. The smallest bird sings. Haven't you ever been to church for God's sake?"

"But what then?" She tried to wrest free willing her mind against the leathery cocoon of wings. They tightened drawing her close with claws at the edges threatening menacingly.

"Eternal sleep," he replied.

"You mean I'd be dead don't you?"

"Eternal salvation is your reward," he uttered.

"I don't want to be saved," she practically screamed silently. "I want to, to live!" She said aloud weakly.

"I'd hoped you might. Now sing something light and lovely, stirring, lively if you will and fresh... please."

"I feel faint."

"Hurry now," he urged. "There is not much time..."

"I'm dreaming of a white..." she sang limply before passing out completely.

"Hopeless," he thought, "though she *could* carry a tune and being young had that colorful girlish voice that radiates innocence and excitement. She might do, he'd have to see. An innocent vampire, that's a good one!" He laughed and began half carrying, half dragging the girl trailing a pale leg from her loose fitting dress. Her shoe was lost to thick vines then the sock to fallen twigs and branches encountered along the way. "It made her look even sexier," he thought. Then reaching the edge of the cemetery, he picked her up and carried her to a large central stone edifice, an ancient mausoleum. It was built for some long dead noble plantationer, slave trader what have you whose withered remains had long since crumbled to be mixed with the earth, his earth. A vampire is never long without his precious earth. He laid her down on one of the many nearby horizontal slabs embedded in the ground around the mausoleum and was soon met by two others. Both acquaintances of many years and wearing black, one a long coat, the other a shorter cape.

"So you finally decided to save one..."

"We were thinking you might be perverted after all those stories and no results!" Said the caped one.

"Sure perverted as any child thinking about sex," he said staring down at her sprawling shapely form. "That's what all of them are just before death, children. With their paltry few years of existence to their credit and what do they think of just before the end, nothing but sex with their husbands or boyfriends... to me, as if they were mere children thinking of it, really."

"Prostitutes treat you better every time!" Added the long coated vampire.

"I wouldn't have wanted her to think of me that way after only a couple minutes. She had only innocence and innocent things in her mind at the time," he said.

"Looks can be deceiving can't they then," said the caped one. "I haven't seen many nicer dresses. You can't ask for more cleavage!" They laugh. "Her hair fragrant as flowers, looks like pure silk on that stone. The one barefoot,

57

the perfect face, a neck to match... who knows what she might have been thinking!" He laughs again.

"I knew what she thought and she can sing like an angel... she may as well be mine! If you've had your fun then you may as well be off. She'll need constant attention for a while I'm sure." He smiled, his fangs protruding slightly. The others depart grudgingly.

"I give it a few decades or so," says the long coated one who laughs then flies off, his coat instantly becoming bat-like webbing.

Dragging her into the mausoleum he notes her body still has slight warmth. He slides the stone lid from the crypt he's chosen. Laying her body inside he curses his forgetfulness not to have inquired about her birth site as some fresh soil will be needed. He hopes it's not far... her accent sounded local. He strokes her hair then bites a small cut on his lip and leaning over allows a drop to splash heavily on her full lips staining them a deep crimson. While kneeling as if praying he whispers to her quietly, "lullaby and goodnight, my love."

A Fly by Night Operation

"What do you think we're running here, a country club?" Startled, the old man looked up from his waiting room chair. "Maybe what we need is some new blood. How old are you anyway Pops? You're real age, not what you tell the government to keep 'em from hunting you down and putting you in a museum?"

"A hundred and eighty three..."

"One eighty three? I'd have sworn you weren't a day over a hundred seventeen! I guess all those wrinkles come in handy don't they when someone you're age feels the need to lie, eh Pops? They make it a little hard to detect the real you, don't they?"

"I could lie just as good when I was younger!"

"That's what I want to hear, a little spirit! Spunk from the old man! Now how about a little work? I didn't hire you for company, my wife gives me all of that I can handle, too much in fact. After ten years with her I wouldn't mind living a couple lifetimes alone, not at all. You're alone aren't you, I bet you feel the same way?"

"I never met..."

"Don't say it! That's about the oldest joke in the world, a joke about the boss's wife. If you knew her you'd want to live alone, don't doubt it! Just be glad you haven't. You'll be lucky if you never do!"

"I was only going to say I haven't met the right woman."

"Don't worry there's still time... hundred and eighty three. And about the other, you know the work... just show up with the bats and you'll do fine. I know that special talent of yours is actually worth good money. Bat catching! Can you believe it, I've hired a bat catcher? If you can bring a few back every night, that's all I ask. You gotta understand though if we were a big commercial company we'd be using sophisticated setups, big nets, the works, and then you'd be out of a job. So just relax there's zoos everywhere that want bats but not too many, that's where we come in. And you get you're Social Security besides when it's slow don't you? I mean they haven't stopped it because you're too old or anything have they?" The old man shook his head. "Of course not," the boss continued. "That'd be a first wouldn't it?"

The old man left the office. It was early evening and the New Mexican horizon shown a brilliant crimson covered with deeper and deeper shades of azure blues. He headed south for the caves with his old truck and a few wire mesh cages in the back. He'd already had cages of his own, and the wild animals he'd caught helped him keep a fresh supply of blood on hand. Cows were of course more manageable and preferred but expensive to maintain. He hoped this new job would change that allowing him to afford the higher quality feed that could quickly fortify a weakened anemic cow's blood. Then he'd be in the pink.

He didn't care much for the boss but cringed whenever he thought how sickly looking his cow had become. Besides he hadn't worked for many months, so now it was time again. An aging vampire has special needs! Social Security and a four hundred dollar monthly check simply couldn't cover them. He was surprised when he'd seen the bat catcher ad in the local newspaper, but a little less than amused when he'd learned the salary. Still he'd been hired, probably because he had his own truck and didn't need any extra equipment. Who was he kidding, who else but a vampire would want to get this close to bats? He should have held out for more. Maybe after he'd proved his worth... not likely with this boss. He knew the type. He'd been around this part of the country long enough to know...

He arrived at a cavern's mouth. They were hard to detect from above being almost entirely subterranean networks, sometimes just spaces in the rocks large enough for families to latch onto walls and ceilings and still fly by without batting each other into the mucky guano down below. He wondered if that experience might not be overly disgusting to them but then the avoidance of predators was probably of primary importance to the smaller species particularly. The old man waited patiently for their emergence a short distance from the opening. He'd also situated himself near a desert shrub and as the rush of small bodies hurled themselves skyward in erratic flight a few took notice of him and were attracted.

Curious, they landed on his clothes, even one on his head, and several others perched clinging upside down to small branches in the shrub. He quickly collected them and placed them in a mesh cage which provided plenty of upside down perches and covered the cage with a large sac of dark cloth. He treated them kindly and held a certain affinity for them. He was sure they felt the same for him. Theirs was the form most easily and readily adaptable in flight. As well their sense of hearing and direction rivaled his own. And something about their chirping and cute velvet fuzziness was somehow irresistible and served to foster a strong innate bond between them. He had simply called to them, and they'd responded. He hoped they'd be well cared for.

When he returned to the office he instructed the boss on their special care and handling though he pretended to already know. This variety was insectivorous and so would need a ready supply of meal worms, maggots or something similarly accessible as there wasn't room to go after their food in the air as is their normal habit. "No flying food, got it!" Said the boss. "I know a pet store place that sells crickets. 'Probably let me have them at a discount in bulk!"

"Very good then," said the old man.

The months passed and the boss true to his word, managed to find and ship to many zoos from different areas interested in exhibiting bats. These zoos built heated glass enclosures for them in the northern climes with windows to their cave world. And the bat caves were at specially darkened locations in the exhibit, though only bright or direct light appeared to agitate them in their cave environs.

The old man was pleased he could help people learn more about bats firsthand while obtaining safe and healthy homes for representative species as well. He made special trips to more remote sites on the wing himself even all the way to Mexico's interior in search of different species. He shocked the boss on occasion bringing in bizarre finds such as very large, three foot long fruit bats and flying foxes. The boss dutifully paid him but he imagined only a fraction of what the zoo would pay, and certainly far below what could be expected as travel expense.

Instead of commendations and compliments he would more usually find himself chastised for being late as he was in a habit of over sleeping on nights during the full moon or after daylight savings time. He liked the work though so he stayed on and the boss soon caught on to an idea selling bats to various research industries. They could be used to test cosmetics similar to rabbits and due to extensive skin surface of the wings proved even more advantageous. Similarly they were mammalian and therefore closer to the human line of evolution than most research animals except monkeys and the apes.

Bats were naturally of particular interest in the field of otoneurology, their advanced central nervous system development important in regards to hearing for echo-location and might have future human applications researchers reasoned... The boss promised to supply the largest bat ears available! Pet stores were also interested as bats unlike birds will not flap about senselessly in a cage. They realize there's no place to go so tend to just hang calmly, probably due to their more evolved mammalian brains. Fortunately for bats the customers who might buy them were not so easily convinced of their adaptability as pets being as they are almost completely nocturnal.

Then by chance the old man was hunting one night and discovered that the bats he'd found this night were not the cute and docile insectivorous or fruit eating varieties but vampires! They didn't land affectionately but with a strong tendency to nip at him at the earliest opportunity. He used this to some advantage since his skin was so leathery that he had difficulty detecting the presence of the tiny furry bodies until they decided to bite. Sometimes with other varieties they'd fly off before they could be collected but with the vampires the sharp vicious little bites instantly alerted him to their presence. Soon however the novelty of collecting the vampires wore off and he went back to collecting more friendly species.

Several weeks after the experience he was in the office listening to the boss who was more talkative than usual. He'd been curious how the old man managed to get so much mileage out of the battered truck. He also wanted to know how he was able to locate such exotic creatures as flying foxes usually endemic to Madagascar and tropical jungles of Central America.

"Those are the tricks of my trade, you can't expect me to let others know about them!" The old man replied. The boss would not have understood anyway, so it was better he didn't know.

The boss had done some studying of his own about bats, enough to realize at least their value to his customers. The vampires were rare but apparently in good supply when a colony could be located. And a genetics research and development laboratory with government funding was interested. They discovered something unusual about the blood in the samples he'd mailed and wanted to talk weekly shipments mentioning amounts of six possibly seven figures over the long-term.

Joking, he said, "Well old man I might be able to make your next hundred years worthwhile if you can start bringing in more of those vampires!" The old man cocked his head as an invitation to continue. "Yeah, the government wants them! Could mean some big pay days. *Could* mind you... you can't tell with bureaucrats until they actually put the money in your hands, and sometimes even then!"

The old man said, "I'm surprised you'd tell me if they were worth that much!"

"Well I tried to get the information out of you, remember? But you wouldn't talk!"

The old man smiled beginning to like the boss just a little. "Well why is it they want them anyway? They're aggressive. I can't see how they'd be much use compared with the others in research."

"They said something about their blood you know genetically. Said it looked somewhat human or had human components I think it was but the amazing thing is that the individual blood cells seem practically indestructible like super blood or something. They also said these vampire cells cannibalize other blood. Their blood actually feeds itself directly somehow bypassing things like the stomach, intestines and liver! If you ask me I'd say that sounds like the same way tequila works, eh old man?" He offered the old men a bottle, two-thirds empty already. "Tequila, it can destroy anything in its path. Am I right?"

"I can't drink, I'm sorry. I have a condition," replied the old man.

"I'll say you do! Your condition is to find all the vampires you can or your condition will be unemployed!"

"You know you're right about these bats. They're not like the others," the old man said. "I'll find the vampires but you'll have to use extra care for their special needs. You may have guessed they need blood but not too much, too little or too much and you'll see they'll be aggressive. They'll have to be shipped at night of course and stay covered in cages at all times during daylight."

"Right, right. You think I don't know the routine by now? Who's the boss here anyway? Forget it. Go on and bring 'em in. I'll have their blood ready. Cow blood good enough?" The old man nodded and left in the truck heading out across the desert, dust billowing up in great clouds as he went.

For weeks they collected and shipped the pug-nosed hostile little devils. They seemed aggressive regardless of how often they were fed but only plates with enough blood to cover the flat surface were used and they never went more than a full day without. The boss utilized heavy gloves when handling the sneering beasts in their small cages while the old man continued his method of letting them bite so he could snatch them when most vulnerable to capture. Or sometimes he snared them in his own large leathery wings if they were reluctant to land. He naturally healed quickly being a vampire and their small stings were of little consequence when compared to earning more than double his usual salary. He was not getting wealthy but he could afford to keep a few cows in hay and have a ready supply of blood for his own special needs.

Then one day it happened, a shipment of angry vampires was late reaching the airport shipping hangar and the next day was bad weather at the destination airport, no planes would be flying there for days. The storm system was stationary for the present. An inspector checking the stowed shipments in New Mexico noted the crated cages of flapping bats which obviously contained live bats although the labels just announced 'live.' He'd removed the covering material briefly and discovered their agitation when exposed to the light of day (the hangar's artificial lighting), and the lack of care. Quarantine wasn't a problem in this instance but regulations required that animals be held no more than a day in hangar awaiting transit, an animal rights provision. These bats had already been held more than three and so would have to be returned to ensure their survival. They seemed hungry though he was unsure how he'd sensed this as he'd never seen real bats before. Their faces actually *looked* hungry, their eyes fixed in his direction.

The crate was returned to the small office by late afternoon. The boss fumed about the airport's 'messed up scales' as he assumed the problem was inadequate postage, not noticing the inspector's 'extended delay hazardous to live animals' notice. They'd be wanting a meal. He wondered how many might need to have the old man's 'special care' before they'd be ready for reshipping? As he pried back the crating wood, they stirred. The small amount of sedative given with the blood for their flight had certainly worn off. The rays of the late afternoon sun dimmed to early evening. The boss noticed he'd nicked his fingers at several points while loosening the crate. No, the nasty little vampires had managed to nick him somehow through the cages. "That did it..." He felt dazed. "Damn their special needs!" He'd let the old man attend to them when he showed up. "If they behaved they could have been lapping up a nice plate of blood right now," he thought. He felt strange. Then he almost changed his mind about the blood plate as if being directed by someone or something. He turned back toward the bats, carrying their plate of blood...

They had already completely pried back the retaining clips to the cage doors when the boss attempted to place the plate in the cage. They were on him almost before his hand could undo the latch, drinking him dry in minutes. His screams wanton music to the hot beat of their flapping webbing as they balanced maintaining positions on the quivering body.

The old man opened the door to the office over which rested the boss's engraved sign, 'A Fly by Night Operation.' They flew by him with blinding speed, about a dozen or two, he couldn't tell... hurrying to suckle at the breast of their warm mother night. He already knew what he'd find when at last he spied the sprawled inanimate bloodless body. He could only exclaim, "well damn him and his whole operation!"

A Red Rose for My Lover

Red, the color of blood, the color of roses, the color of love... could it be any other?

There once was a man whose lover chose to wear nothing but red. Red dresses, red suits... after a few weeks he was completely put out. He asked himself what did it mean, this obsession, almost a perversion for red? Maybe she'd tell him he reminded her of a lover she'd known before, someone who'd frightened her so she thought to wear red at all times. So she might therefore remind him of her mortality, her frailty that could result in a broken body with real blood if he was not careful to exert more control.

What is love if not obsession, possessed of certain demons and perhaps a little too real at times to suit the tastes of most normal people? If he were a bull of a man he might have been enraged at the sight of so much red. Fortunately for her his physique tended to range between slight and frail though exercise and a more healthy body may have helped him achieve a healthier mind as well. While a sage men tends to approach life with moderation the insane drives past the edges of extreme. All his energies it seemed focused only on her, and like the bull he often ran to extremes.

Oh to be young again in years, mortal and in love. He could hardly imagine it now but he once was in love with love, the very idea of being in love with such an attractive girl. That he'd found her then at that crucial time in life was reason enough to have become well, insane.

Gyrelle could drive most men to distraction. It was not so much her physical beauty though. Her hair was extremely long, dark and flowing, and her body possessed of interestingly intricate curves. He also desired her mind of course, and knew he couldn't have one without the other. Such were the times back then whereas today a girl might often give her body without emotional attachments and vice versa. A gage of a society's maturity might depend on the variety of social liaisons it produces. But in older times centuries past the church for one exerted rather strict control over most social practices hence a young girl's love tended to be an all or none proposition for the suitors rivaling for her attention.

While competition is often a healthy thing among men engaged in sport or business, with love however they revert quickly to children. Little did he realize he might have an eternity to play at these games with her. Her mortal suitors would fall away into the musty years of time. And in time all would be forgotten, all else save himself. Eventually she'd see the size of his passion and ardor and not deny him. Only she could free him from the madness, let him up from the pit of hell, his Gyrelle.

One cool evening she was out on the veranda of the stately house watching as the breeze swayed the spanish moss which clung delicately draping itself among all the large tree limbs and she saw him. She would often sit alone on the porch enjoying the night air near the plants in the window well. Some nights, there'd be unusual stirrings from the garden, perhaps rats readying themselves for a night's foraging on unsecured garbage. Maybe there were even larger animals out there roaming about scenting the air for the unmistakable fragrance of her sweet perfume before following the rats to a buffet of refuse. Then there he was in the darkest corner partially obscured by a tree, just standing and watching her. The wind through his garments made the unmistakable sound she'd been hearing. She strained her eyes to recognize him but could not. If she were to tell of this to her father he would probably charge out with his long gun and kill the man. She now realized she would have to soon heed the attentions of her suitors for the proper protection from strange encounters... Her gaze momentarily diverted she returned it to the tree but the man had gone.

That week she finally decided to entertain the affections of one of several suitors who had often come inquiring of her time. She had never really obliged one before and usually after some weeks or months they would stop only to be replaced by some others to take up the cause anew or so it seemed to her. The one she chose was an infrequent visitor but had been at it a longer duration of time overall than most. He also had a quirky smile and manner of gait.

He smiled broadly when she told him of her decision. They talked a short while and she made a date for that next evening. He said he would buy a new suit of clothes and return with flowers for his Gyrelle. She learned he obsessed over meeting her since seeing her in town once laughing with a group of girls, her friends from school days. She hid the matter of the date from her parents. The next evening he arrived promptly with a rose and insisted they take his coach to town and then a walk as was the habit with young people desiring to show themselves off.

He returned her home and she insisted he stay. She invited him to sit with her on the veranda. They talked of stupid and silly things, nursery rhymes, favorite pets, what their parents thought of various crimes, that her favorite color was red... He invited her to walk behind the garden with him. She was hesitant but he assured her things would be all right with him near. The sky was cloudy and the night even darker than it was before when she'd seen the man. They walked to the dark corner of the garden and when they reached the tree he embraced her strongly and they kissed which surprised her. But when she did not immediately resist he took this as an overture to love and proceeded to bring her down to the soft moss covered earth. He forced her to remove her undergarments and helped by ripping some in the effort. She didn't dare cry out to alert her parents of the predicament and her embarrassment but suffered quietly the fulfillment of the young man's wanton lust. He told her at the finish that he was glad it'd happened as now they'd have to be married if she wanted to remain decent and that it was something he needed to do however long it may have taken her to prepare for it. Besides he loved her and that was what really mattered. She left him without a word and when she looked back to him, she realized to her horror he'd been the man behind the tree as she watched him standing silhouetted as before against that tree.

He returned the next day and all the next week but was turned away every time. He left a red rose for her at the each visit but couldn't know if they'd been delivered, until finally she answered personally and admonished him not to return, that she would not accept his call.

I confess to being confused and in a deep despair at that time, choosing to forsake my usual work and routine, and instead spending much of that time wandering the cemeteries in the same suit of clothes. Occasionally I'd stop to rest and recline on the large slabs of stone and marble for the strange comfort they seemed to offer. After a few weeks of this I became weakened and lingered resting longer into evening, having little interest in food or living in general.

It was about at that time I judge I was bitten. I can't be exactly sure when as I was not aware of it at the time, but that it was a vampire there can be no doubt. I manifested all the usual symptoms. I then took up residence in the cemetery and used my powers to obtain what wealth and blood I needed. I continued to stalk and visit Gyrelle even long after she'd already married. She never allowed herself to entertain my company again though. I noticed that she did have a preference for wearing the color red rather often which reminded me of when we talked on her veranda. I liked to try to imagine different sorts of reasons it was her favorite, not the least of which was that she'd become a vampire herself... She seemed to such a natural way about her, the look of one.

I am at last convinced she has indeed joined the ranks of the undead herself. I'm not sure when it may have happened... but she will not heed my hypnotic call as others, the living, do. Still, being a vampire should only make her more sensitive to my presence and desires. Yet all remains as it did, unchanged.

It has been many years now and we have not aged. I imagine she may hold her grudge to the end which could be a very longtime. I think I'll leave this place now but before I do I'll visit one last time and leave a red rose for my lover...

You Know He's a Vampire When...

Since earliest times there have been vampires who set themselves apart, who watch and judge others of their kind. They protect society from the actions of the maniacs which in turn affords other vampires protection, the anonymity they need to survive... This is a story of one such slayer and the 'renegade' he must bring to justice. Unlike the slayer's counterpart in human society, the detective policeman, he is not only sure of the perpetrator's guilt, but that he is also a vampire. And since capture isn't a viable option the slayer feels vindicated carrying out his sentence, execution if you will... Slayers, it's a tradition as old as vampirism and some might say, who would begrudge a man, or vampire, the performance of his civic duty? Unrecognized and for the most part, unrewarded, they provide a service nonetheless to those who might value their mortal lives, their souls, or the glint of sunlight on flowers growing in a park. And I don't just mean cemetery parks!

Oh by the way our slayer's name is John and works for the L.A.P.D., the perpetrator's name, well I guess we'll call him the perpetrator for now.

John

"They say time loves a hero... What have you got to show for your five hundred?"

Perpetrator

"Just cause I say I'm the oldest I suppose... You want me to prove

73

something?"

John

"No, I was just wondering if you had already..."

Perpetrator

"I think I've proved insomnia a virtue. It's made me what I am and yourself as well."

John

"That doesn't count. Insomnia's natural for a vampire."

Perpetrator

"Would you be amused if I told you I preferred the day? I'm actually what you'd call a 'reverse' vampire. Coffee makes me sleep, aspirin gives me a headache, things like that..."

John

"Maybe you're not a vampire at all?"

Perpetrator

"Yeah, maybe you're just an informer, or what do you call them... slayers? Maybe I'm really a wacked-out vampire groupie spending my life searching for drugs and a chance at immortality."

John

"Well you show up at my favorite dining spot also conveniently a few short blocks from my favorite seedy nightclub and dressed like that, it's hard to say what you might be... What are those, wood sandals and beach khakis and a black velvet shirt with a glow in the dark moon, a nice touch. Most traditional vampires wear clothes from the time periods they lived."

Perpetrator

"I know the original clothes have a more protective effect, sure it's easier to transform but I'm not your traditional vampire. I like the younger crowd as do you or you wouldn't be here, would you? Only Gothic cultist types get into the frills and lace of sixteenth century formal wear."

John

"You've got a point and you do have impressive teeth. If I hadn't noticed them right off we might have been forced to engage in a life or death struggle, an immortal conflict if you will..."

Perpetrator

"I could say the same though women are my exclusive prey."

John

"I should have guessed from the stories in the papers..."

Perpetrator

"Guilty as charged. Hey I know a way we can be sure about each other. How about a sip, just a small one... I know when to say when."

John

"You are young then aren't you? You wouldn't want to run the risk of drinking unclean blood would you?"

Perpetrator

"Well you know I have heard some... horror stories but personally no, I haven't had the problems. I do however prefer the strong tonics though, a young girl completely soused or strung out. God that's what it's about isn't it? They call it paradise... I don't know why." He whistles the Eagles hit tune gaily through his fangs, a sound akin to wind across marsh reeds.

John

"Bite your tongue. How can you say that?"

Perpetrator

"It's true they don't live long with me around. 'Just a habit."

John

"Worse than smoking I'd say!"

Perpetrator

"You think you know a lot, let me touch your... yeah the wrist will do. Cold as ice, no pulse. I guess so, what do you know!"

John

"I can get whatever you want you know... for your girls. Drugs, just name your poison!"

Perpetrator

"Sure."

John

"Wait, let me get this down. You say you'd like 20 grams.... for you're girl."

Perpetrator

"That's right, I like what it does to her blood. Yeah and if it's not right I'll know."

John

"Then you'll hunt me down and..." He takes out his pad and pen.

Perpetrator

"Man what do ya think you're writing about? What do they call you the drug dork?"

John

"'Just like to know who I'm dealing with. There's no name so... just making a few notes so I don't forget what you look like."

Perpetrator

"So what do you want for it anyway, part of the action I'd bet?"

John

"I'll let you know."

Perpetrator

"Well then anything addicting is fine, the wanker the better. It also helps the police close a case when that's involved, less cause for alarm. Helps 'em dot the T's and cross the eyes you unnerstand." He crosses his eyes.

John

"Here's a card with my address, drop by tomorrow night and I'll have something ready for you."

Perpetrator

"Hey sounds good. I'll wear my tie! Ha, just kidding... John (looking at card). Call me Ishmael. Nah, a joke. 'Name's Raymond!"

John

"Gotcha, (pointing as if finger were a gun)."

John

(meanwhile back at the stakeout)

"He took it all, hook, line and sinker... just like we planned!"

Joe

"If you say so Lieutenant... as long as we get the scumbag off the streets."

John

"I could have been his next but luckily he's got an aversion to male blood!"

Joe

"If you say so, sounds sick either way to me though."

John

"You're not a vampire Joe, that's just the way it goes. You'll see when he shows up."

Joe

"I'm glad it's anything goes with this character, John. Imagine ten girls dead in as many weeks in the same area. He'll get the full clip (patting his gun) before he has the chance to try to pull something with us. So not that I care really but why do you think he acts like a vampire?"

John

"I don't think he can help it, Joe."

Joe

"At least he'll be an easy mark then. What does he have, the whole routine with black cape and pointy teeth and all?"

John

"Maybe, but he said he might wear a tie. 'Said his name was Raymond. He practically admitted the killings though he didn't come right out and say it, but he did some things as DeNiro might say..."

Joe

"He said he was a vampire though, right?"

John

"Yea, a couple times..."

Joe

"That's good enough for me if he wants to admit to the M.O., which just happens to be the same one used by our serial killer! Pretty stupid if you ask me..."

John

"Madmen have been known to be strong so... "

Joe

"Don't worry he won't get the chance."

John

"Shhh! Joe, I think he's coming!"

Joe

"I don't hear anything..." (then a few moments later the sounds of light steps in the hallway, knock, knock.)

Raymond

"It's me, John, open up. Or I'll huff and puff and blow the house in. You know the routine!" (He laughs.)

John

"It's already open, Ray, come in."

Raymond

"I hear ya, nice place, kind of dark though, (laughing). Say who's this?" (He notices Joe pointing his gun.)

Joe

"Alright hands up and don't move!"

Raymond

"Is this what happens when you trust a vampire, well you won't get the others. My girls are safe, pig."

Joe

"Your girls are dead aren't they Mr. Vampire, just like you'll be if you make one move!"

Raymond

"Not those girls, they're not my girls. They were just for fun. I wouldn't expect you to understand."

Joe

"I understand that you make one false move and you're history!"

Raymond

"That's a good one! And just how am I supposed to put up my hands if I don't move, huh? Maybe like this?" (Raymond raises his hands and flies across the room at Joe who reacts quickly emptying his clip.)

Joe

"Sheesh! That was stupid! Did you see that? He came right at me with his bare hands. 'Must've hit him ten times. You okay John? Hey what are you doing? What the!"

John

"It's gotta be done before he..."

Joe

"Before he what? You're not going to really drive a stake through his... Jesus Christ! The guy was still alive, incredible. But I don't think he would've been much longer, John. What do you think he meant about his other girls...? Maybe he's got more hostages."

John

"I don't think so, probably a gang of occult followers. If he's the only murderer we probably won't have to worry too much about them. When they find their leader and supplier is missing they'll probably get straight. Hey don't touch that stake. Leave it in a while."

Joe

"He looks different a little older now, Christ... I don't believe it, John."

John

"Kind of makes you want a believe in something doesn't it?" (The corpse withers to dust before their eyes.) "You know they're vampires when they do things like that."

You Know My Name, Look Up The Number

"I know it's much too nice a night to be attending a Dater's Anonymous meeting. Who wouldn't rather be out on a date than in a stuffy classroom listening to someone like me drone on about the hazards and pitfalls, correction the abyss of failure and intimidation waiting to swallow us the moment we try to feel affection for someone else. Am I right?" The small group offers a smattering of applause.

"But do we give up?"

"No!" returns the class en mass.

"No, or we wouldn't be here! Each of us are sharing, competent, integral members of society. Some are no doubt caring professionals, others are perhaps less caring or professional then we'd want to admit concerning our jobs but what matters most, I'm sure we'll all agree, is that crucial social contact." Some renewed applause is heard.

"Mixing with our common man or woman is what we need. We crave it and it won't be denied! Am I right?"

"Right!" Replies the class in unison.

"But there are problems, as any indiscriminate dater knows. Many of the problems we've heard in past weeks have been big problems, but not insurmountable I'd wager. And those of you who've already been married will probably agree that it is the small problems, or the most trivial annoyances to

81

one or both partners, that most often lead to divorce down the road. Our concern then is to make those small things, the petty inconveniences into big things now while we're dating and ready for them and so make our mistakes early before real damage results. I know we haven't touched on the topic of marriage before but I'm sure everyone realizes it is a very real possibility, an eventual outcome that every dater must face." The group erupts with brief applause in response. Someone, a girl in the front, raises a hand...

"Yes Sheila?"

"I think your methods are keeping me neck deep in problems. I'm so confused I think I'll be dating forever!"

"Well you may want to just stop, if only for a while and take inventory. After all we wouldn't call ourselves 'Dater's Anonymous' if we advocated nonstop dating, would we?"

"That's right," chime in some other group mates.

"Well, personally I can't stop. I need the sex, you know the physical attraction. I guess I'm the opposite of frigid, what do you call it? Larvae?" says Sheila.

"Nymph, nympho..." someone shouts. The group laughs.

"Yes Sheila, we're all well aware of the problems you've been having with your last boyfriend but I thought we agreed that sex is the one area we would leave to silent communication. The subtleties of a touch or expression can be much more appropriate initially than open discussion or frankly asking for it, the sex that is."

"I know but I'm just not satisfied, you know? I could probably have five boyfriends and it'd be the same."

"Then this is where you belong, but tonight I think we should hear from a new member first and let that insight help us each in its own way."

Before he can continue someone from the back asks, "who wants to know how many boyfriends Sheila has?" The others clap while she raises at hand in indicating four with her fingers.

"I see we have a new member today so before we start let me emphasize that Sheila is something of an extremist, with a sleeping libido seemingly awake at all the wrong hours. Some might describe her as difficult, hardened or recalcitrant but we're not here to call each other names." Some applause and snickering... "We're not after her to change!" More applause. "We all want the same thing, that inner peace so easily destroyed, so elusive and overlooked but worth every effort to find."

"Other members have had problems no less severe. Bob approaches dating like germ warfare bringing a full arsenal of disinfectants, soaps, towels and wet wipes to each encounter..." The group laughs. "John needs to vigorously berate and demean his partner in order to feel any physical attraction. And at least to this point he's managed to evade any lawsuits or jail time." Some coughing and a little clapping. "Sally can only be with drunk men. Sandy has to lie. Richard never dates the same girl twice. Tom stopped dating for the time being and couldn't be happier." Tom nods. "The list continues doesn't it? So those of you who are newcomers, while daytime talk-shows may offer a one time deal to their guests our group goes on until the cure or marriage, sometimes both if we're lucky!" Some laughter.

"Let me call on you if I might, Vlad is it from your name tag, to give us a brief state of affairs, real or imagined, fact or even fiction. We've all been there and that's why we're here, to help! And please say your own name and address yourself as a dater... our only requirements."

"Er yes," replies Vlad clearing his throat and wiping his lips on the back of one hand. "You've pronounced it correctly. My name is Vlad, Vladimir actually. I'm sorry the folds of the cloak have obscured the rest." He pauses for some coughing from the group. "And I am a dater!" There is steady applause among the group, then just scattered clapping, then quiet.

"Go on Vlad what problem brings you, a man of obvious stature and physical bearing, to us?"

"I don't know really. I have a lot to offer and am not unattractive in the bargain yet they never call. I meet them all the time at bars or after a show, perhaps shopping, anywhere really, girls who seem interested... you know and we'll talk. Sometimes I'll mention that I can control the forces of darkness, or even offer them immortality. It seems to work fine for a while and I'll leave them a number usually after a quick bite. Then a week, two, three go by and nothing. I thought I might have picked up some rare contagion, or virus causing amnesia of some sort. Because though I choose to leave the choice with them, on occasion I've been the one to call only to find there is apparent role playing of either avoidance or complete ignorance going on, the *cold shoulder* as it's known. It's maddening really to someone of my... stature as you put it. If they ever knew the full extent of my power they would..." He pauses.

"What do you think they'd do Vlad?"

"I know what they'd do. I've seen it often enough. There'd be a lot of cowering, whimpering, carrying on... you know, crying, and at least in the old days... complete submission."

"And this complete submission would involve some sort of sex then, any routine or style preferred? Excuse me for breaking my own rule about sex talk, but we can make an exception in this case, can't we class?" The class voices it's approval. Sheila looks dejected.

"Well I doubt if that makes a difference really, but of course necking is fairly typical..."

"You mentioned something about controlling the forces of nature and powers over life and death. So you want to invite young girls to your laboratory where you might experiment on them and give them a concoction, potent drugs possibly, that would convince them of your power? Very interesting so far Vlad. I'm just hoping though this fixation or *quirk* as we tend to call our dating desires here is not a metaphor for something more sinister, say your power over life and death. It's a lot to think about so just take a moment to consider if that's what you really want."

"No really I don't, not anymore at least. Yes before long ago, centuries really, if you knew you could take a girl by force you'd take her. Why not? They didn't know what they were feeling and could scarcely understand it if they did. And I don't have a laboratory and drugs or anything like that... Controlling the forces of darkness is just that, my powers. I thought with all the shows these days about Batman and the others..." He flaps his cloak imperiously.

"Superman?"

"Kind of I suppose but..."

"The point I'm trying to make Vlad is believability, confidence, trust. With someone of you're obvious strong character and imposing presence... I'd say go-ahead. Go with what works. If it worked in the past, do it again. But in the face of our old acquaintance, failure, which you describe comically in terms of *centuries*, well we have to make a change don't we? Does anyone else see something of a pattern here? Yes, Sheila?"

"Oh, I was scared at first, kind of. Your whole manner is very mysterious though and that's very sexy of course. If you could lighten up a little, not treat it like a life or death subject I think you'll get some calls. And if it's okay I'd like to call you, Vlad. Necking is my favorite too!" She bats her eyes at him. He gazes at her hypnotically.

"So Vlad and Sheila then, there's a pair class!" The class greets the announcement with applause. Promise us though we won't be reading anything wild and crazy in the newspapers."

"Oh I think Vlad and I might be busy trading stories... (pause) I give us at least a week before there's anything in the news!" The class laughs at Sheila's prediction. Vlad grins at her.

Blood From a Stone

Often in the course of human events there arise stories that are for lack of a better word, weird... supernatural, superstitious stories that are better left untold. Some may want to think of aliens, magic or witches when faced with the unknown and they may be right but to those who were witness, the following particular instance at least can only be attributed to the work of a vampire.

The following events happened many years ago and though I've told a few friends this is the first written record. I made my living in those days as a journalist for a mid-sized city newspaper. My editor let me travel a lot, sending me to mainly rural areas to cover special interests, curiosities or carnival events and the like. It was considered bad taste to simply copy local news reporting at some times while standard practice at others. Sometimes there'd be trouble if a local paper was respected or popular enough to invoke the word plagiarism and then all hell would break loose at the office. So my job was usually thought of as important, at least as far as our reputation. The actual stories on the other hand were at best only of nominal or passing interest to most and as I've already said, weird.

Before I left on assignment I was reminded by my editor to make nice with the townsfolk for as always there would be politics to consider. I would be the paper's representative, an ambassador to other media and journalists who may be present. If it was healthy to doubt one's editor then I was in peak condition and reminded him in turn that 'the story's the thing' and that I wasn't covering any election this trip. It was a rather unique relationship I had with my editor that allowed us to each think the other senile and still function as a team.

The actual nature of the event was a kind of unofficial strong man contest something akin to the caper toss in Scotland only without capers naturally. Also an historical house would be toured, one built from imported stone and housing many worthwhile authentic artifacts or so read the invitation.

The trip was uneventful and I reached the rural Virginia town of Dunsworth two days early in order to gain a little background information for the article. The scenery was beautiful as are most settings before the ravages of civilization are allowed to take hold. Dunsworth was essentially a one street town and I found the people friendly and cooperative though uninformed about the contest and its host, a mysterious recluse.

Some of course pretended to be informed in the way country people often do but most admitted they'd never seen the owner and were only vaguely familiar with the great stone residence nearby. Apparently few had actually seen the house as it was adjudged to be anything from a mansion to a small cottage in size. That it was strangely constructed and haunted was without question however and inaccessible from the road and protected by dogs. There had been no real incidents except the occasional scared curious child so things were pretty much left alone. The town drunk had claimed to have spent lost days at the place but his stories went unconfirmed except to help the rumor of its being haunted. When I asked, if the place were haunted why hadn't it been reported to the national media, I was surprised to hear that it had been only that 'the Yankees were afraid to come.'

The house in question was then placed well within the category of *weird* but I'd need actual proof before I could actually feel afraid. At most I felt only a little timid. After all there'd been no incidents and no well-defined superstitious talk to ward me off. To be on the safe side though I took with me the standard protections against evil... religious charms, a small Bible and a tablecloth imprinted with the sign of the holy sepulcher from the town church. I reasoned that if they were going to scare me they shouldn't mind the loan of a few precautions. I also ate a liverwurst sandwich loaded with onions as I read somewhere once that wild animals are repelled by the strong scent of pungent herbs.

The invitation's directions led me to a trail off the main road and only just outside town. Since Dunsworth was so small the trail was within walking distance from the hotel which helped me feel a little safer. Unfortunately the trail itself was long and not able to accommodate a car. Being thirty hours early I could take my time but soon reconsidered the enterprise when I came upon a tall stone wall and heavy wrought iron gate. I had already decided to head back when I heard the first wolf. It emitted a low moaning dog-like sound that slowly transformed in quality to the typical wolf howl usually only observed on late-night horror movies. Then there were other calls more distant in answer to the first. I hoped but couldn't be sure they were on the other side of the wall so I quickly trotted back along the trail. When I returned to the hotel and related my experience at the downstairs bar I was greeted as a kind of daring explorer then left abruptly alone. I suppose in their eyes I'd already done something foolish. Then what would it be like tomorrow I wondered?

I would have my answer soon enough. The function was set for 6 pm. or roughly dusk. I spent my remaining waking hours worrying whether my host had received my reply to the RSVP. If he had not and I'd be the only stranger present, say as an official of sorts merely needed for the purposes of documenting some esoteric ritual, then their dogs might be loose to keep strangers such as myself away. They'd make quick work of me of that there'd be no doubt. Maybe there really had been wolves, untamed wild wolves waiting for a feeding their wolf nature told them intuitively would come. The more I thought about the wolves the less I liked my chances. I began to remember books I'd read as a child that had contained or been about wolves and despised the authors for having written so vividly. I finally convinced myself that my silver bladed pocket knife might be enough backup protection even in the event of werewolves after I'd downed several large ales at the hotel bar. As I got up to leave the local drunk who'd been sitting nearby whispered that I need not fear the children of the night, that they would guide me well. Then he winked and bared his teeth in a half snarl. I don't know what frightened me more, the condition of his teeth or that he was trying to imitate a wolf but I left hurriedly on foot cursing my editor with every step.

I arrived at the trail just as the sun abandoned its post on the horizon, its absence infecting the air with an eerie chill. Through spaces in the trees I could already see clouds racing by the bright face of the moon and looking ahead the path appeared to be almost shimmering with reflected moonlight. Was I taking special notice of things because I was about to die or just trying to stall for like reason? I couldn't decide but my senses were heightened, sinuses clear and vision unusually sharp even among the shadows. Then I noticed them, wolves, their large yellow eyes and sleek strong bodies moving easily through the trees. They didn't make any sounds this time but appeared at all sides at first walking fast then running spurring me to a gallop until I had almost run headlong into the stone wall. I stopped a moment to catch my breath and noticing the open gate entered to find the wolves now gone. It had been quite awhile since I'd run that far so fast but was surprised to feel the better for it.

I continued along the path and in a few minutes reached the house which was constructed similarly of large stone blocks and shielded mostly by large trees of a type I had not seen before. For some reason I wasn't sure why I thought of the tree in Genesis, 'the tree of the knowledge of good and evil' and half expected to hear the hiss of huge serpents. Instead as I touched the front door a wolf bayed in the nearby woods. Losing composure I began to bang on the door with a closed fist when it quickly opened and I stood confronted with my host.

"Hello young friend and good evening. Come in and welcome to what I call Castle Dunsworth. You may call me Master Dunsworth or Master if you like. Others who have visited from town have called me Mr. Master." He paused to laugh, "but I think that sounds too much like a type of cement, don't you?"

"Why yes, Count." I chuckled. "I mean Master, sorry. You can call me..."

"I know who you are. Your editor has been well compensated to send you."

"Why the... he didn't say anything."

"It's a very important festival for my friends, a first of its kind really, a competition... The contestants will be announced and you are to record events as you see them. How do you feel?"

"I feel exceptionally well considering the running. Do you know that..." Before I could ask him about the wolves he was suddenly gone. His appearance certainly matched his title. He could easily pass for any of those, Master, Count, Duke, Baron... I was glad he hadn't taken offense when I'd toyed with his name. But it almost seemed as if he anticipated my curiosity regarding his 'children of the night' when he'd disappeared.

Other than my introduction with the Master the evening proceeded rather slowly, boringly I could say. There were about a dozen others in attendance I'd noted. Most appeared to be men of means and wearing dark long coats or capes cut of luxuriant fabrics, completely out of place for this time of year I thought. None were known to me nor showed much interest in myself or my questions as if I were on par with a butler or servant, which in a way I suppose I was. But I wasn't about to let them feel the better of the situation so I remained aloof shunning them as they did me. I studied the artwork placed about the main hall and waited.

Presently the Master entered the room and announced the imminent start of the competition. He said, "I hope you all fed well in recent days to be at your peak strength. Remember, ours is a race of dominance and authority. Let him who's heart proves strongest be so assigned his rightful place of order." There was mutual agreement with this and urging to proceed from his guests... "Let's begin but know the rules, there is to be no dining on this night of competition nor fighting or complaints of any kind. Each will have only one chance to raise the stone and our scribe will record and compare results. His decision is final!"

I couldn't help feel a little embarrassed. I knew he was referring to me and my real function was now clear. Each one in turn would be trying to lift the huge slab of stone that rested in the middle of the hall. It was supported at three points by smaller massive stones about a foot in height. The contestant would lie under the big stone and attempt to lift it as high as possible. There was a vertical large-scale ruler conveniently placed on one side that would be used to gauge the results. It was straight forward enough except for one thing, the stone slab was huge, a massive affair about a foot thick, and probably ten feet on each of its four edges. It had to weigh tons... unless the stone was really not stone but some lighter material only resembling stone.

Incredibly though I couldn't doubt the stone was real for as each man in turn went beneath it I heard the grinding of the large stone against its supports and the movements of the stone in the air indicated as much, swaying mightily back and forth until once more coming to rest with loud cracks upon the pedestals. Their efforts were beyond anything I'd ever seen or imagined, and in a word super-human. Or more accurately, not human at all. I did my best to record it all, some managed several inches, others better than a couple feet. They tried various methods from lying supine on their backs and lifting from hands and knees, to using their backs to contact the great slab. Others supported all with just legs or neck and arms. At the end I went to the stone myself just to feel and know from touch what my eyes had seen.

Then before any winner had been announced the men collapsed, one by one and groaning almost as loudly as they had during the lifts. They clutched their chests cursing but muttering about how well they performed and to have the results ready... Why bother I wondered? Even so I had already completed the tally and given the results to the Master who had not participated I'd realized. He gazed over their bodies, strewn about and writhing in pain, some apparently already dead...

"Soon they will be dead..." he said. "In strict medical terms it is called cardiac tamponade, a buildup of blood within the tough sac of sinew surrounding the heart. The heart under such strain will leak, the vessels bursting their walls attempting to penetrate a muscle straining with the strength of twenty or thirty men. The sac then fills, pressing and suffocating the pump."

"Isn't there a cure," I implored, "if you knew this would happen?"

"Yes, only one," he replied, "a sharpened wooden stake squarely over the heart, driven through ribs and spreading them, allowing the pierced sac to drain... It's the only way." Master Dunsworth then preceded to stake each and every one where they lie, only he did not merely puncture the sac I'm sure, but went through and through the hearts themselves. The blood that flowed was terrible. When he finished I asked simply, "Why?"

"I wanted them to die," he said. "You see they were vampires. It's the only way to deal with them you know. You can go now and speak of this if you must, they'll never believe you no matter how good a journalist you are!"

I needed no further hinting that my story had ended and only later when safely within the confines of my office wondered whether the master vampire's prediction was actually a thinly veiled compliment... "no matter how good a journalist you are!" Much more likely it'd been a threat and I'd just been an instrument of convenience. Unfortunately I had much less difficulty interpreting my editor's reaction to the story, one of pure undistilled hostility... "the work of an over active imagination combined with an undeveloped talent," he said. "Next time you get lost in the woods and miss a story just admit it!"

Timetable Blues

Sometimes in the world a coincidence occurs which may be considered rare or even inevitable. Who's to say for sure? About all we know is that they do occur as when old friends meet unexpectedly after many years or lost relatives are reunited by chance, or as in this case... two vampires confront each other over sharing the same compartment on a lonely Carpathian Mountains Line train. One is magnificently old, and the other brash and young.

Young Vampire

"God I hate traveling. So it's compartment 19 again, are you assigned?"

Old Vampire

"Yes damn it, what's the point? I'm going to be here all night just like last night."

Young Vampire

"Well just wondering, you didn't say much... thought maybe you don't speak the language. Do you sleep during the day?"

Old Vampire

"Yeah the same place you do..."

Young Vampire

"Now that you mention it, I did see another coffin back there."

95

Old Vampire

"Yup, a couple stuffy coffins piled under the other baggage on the cargo car..."

Young Vampire

"So you're..."

Old Vampire

"That's right, I didn't sleep good and woke up to see molten gold coming right at me through the window."

Young Vampire

"That hurts... you okay?"

Old Vampire

"You'd think after hundreds of years of existence a vampire'd be able to tell time, maybe a little instinctive intuition regarding time of day..."

Young Vampire

"For me, it's only been a hundred, give or take. Hey I couldn't help notice the ornate cross carvings on yours, the coffin..."

Old Vampire

"A mild concession... I find it helps put a little of the fear of God into the curious."

Young Vampire

"I bet you had a nice funeral service to go with it too..."

Old Vampire

"Alright, I guess I deserved that one. You look so young I bet you've got some wild stories to pass the night."

Young Vampire

"Why don't you go first, something with real horror would be great... maybe your first staking?" He laughs loudly.

Old Vampire

"Oh you want a story, a real horror story? For example, say what if this train we're traveling on derails in a few moments sending a thousand shards of wood and debris hurtling through these compartments... It'd be the luck of the draw wouldn't it? But that's not to your liking I suppose. You only want something documented, horror from the past?"

Young Vampire

"Well if you got it, only if you got it! And you don't have to get so testy. But nothing silly please, say relating to your bad hygiene causing a panic among the masses. You know something only horrible to mortals... You needn't worry offending me. It did at first but I can turn it off, ha!"

Old Vampire

Laughing..."Oh I've plenty of those or how about... A story of the birth of a terrible monster. Imagine this, that you're only comfort might be temperate weather and that you were imprisoned in a frozen waste and that you preferred only one type of food and that it was denied you. Imagine also that you became imprisoned not through lack of strength or the cunning of your enemies but through your own simple stupid miscalculation. How might you feel? Imagine a man trapped for months, can't say exactly as I didn't keep count. But you're in a deep cavern without light or running water and unable to escape due to injuries... due to falling in the place. Your, I mean his only company a small colony of bats or an occasional animal falling into the same trap. His only food, the same, perhaps most often the diseased or cannibalized bats dropping to the cavern's floor no longer with the strength to hold their position on the rock."

Young Vampire

"Horrible... True?"

Old Vampire

"Imagine the prolonged agony of untended broken bones. Their ends refused to knit due to cold and starvation. They instead develop permanent new areas of flexion or extension, as if multiple new small joints had been

97

formed until at long last the limbs could be employed for grasping, clawing and climbing your way to the opening, and sunlight... And there to realize another agony... a first indication you were no longer as other men in more ways than just those of bone and sinew. Of course I'm referring to vampirism or becoming a batman if you prefer the slang of the kids these days... and of course the reason I didn't die in that cave."

Young Vampire

"Unusual transition... real story, actual bats did it? Intriguing, a bona fide vampire strain then?"

Old Vampire

"Apparently so... Perhaps the original strain, pure vampires. Probably forced into unusual climes due to attempts by people to eradicate them... Fed on me as I slept, much as I fed on their injured mates or victims."

Young Vampire

"I wouldn't begrudge you a certain hatred of life, even all things living after a conversion like that!"

Old Vampire

"I would doubt there are any vampires, any of any history, that would say they love their existence. Though just to exist might necessitate such a love at times."

Young Vampire

"Yes I'm well aware. For the moment, I only hope our train's on time. There's nothing I deplore more than a change in timetable, aside from being forced to share a cave with bats!" He laughs. "Excuse me."

Old Vampire

"For me I'm looking forward to dinner. If the menu issued at boarding is right a rare roast beef is to be expected. Oh here's the conductor, I'll ask!"

Conductor

"Hello there, tickets please." He takes the tickets. "Dinner in twenty..."

98

Old Vampire

"Oh may I make a special request regarding the meal, if it's all right?" quickly withdrawing a crooked gnarled arm.

Conductor

"Sure go-ahead, I'll tell the steward."

Old Vampire

"Yes I'd prefer just the juice, you know the blood of beef mainly if I could for sopping with bread you know. I've even brought my own loaf, so please as much as you can spare! I'll pay full price..."

Conductor

"I see, well I'll do what I can... a bit of a savage are we then?" He laughs and departs.

Old Vampire

"No, no we are not! At least not at the moment anyway, but this an occasion isn't it? I could make an exception." He smiles showing some fang... "God I hate that kind of naive serendipity mortals can have where you'd swear they know exactly who or what you are."

Young Vampire

"Yes but you're always reassured in the end aren't you?"

Old Vampire

"They're dolts through and through for the most part I'd say. I could probably have told that conductor I was a doctor and requested he assemble volunteers to donate blood for you my ailing patient."

Young Vampire

"Why didn't you? Or have him collect beef blood for the same purpose, ha. You might even have him announce that there are vampires on board and anyone interested should come back to compartment 19!" Just then the conductor sticks his head back into their compartment and stares at them crazily in an attempt to get a laugh.

99

Conductor

"Oh sorry, may have missed a ticket. May I see yours again?" He looks again at the young vampire, his expression returning to normal after startling him.

Young Vampire

"Sure ah, here it is Mr. Conductor."

Conductor

"Thanks very much, sorry again. Well here's the stewardess with your special order." She enters briefly leaving a large plate of blood on the small fold away table and leaves smiling. The old vampire attempts to lock her gaze in an hypnotic snare but the conductor's interference breaks the spell.

Young Vampire

"Do you think he heard?"

Old Vampire

"Are you kidding of course not. Didn't I just call him a dolt, I would have at least expected a sneer out of him not just a funny face. I'd be more concerned with the stewardess myself... Smiling over a plate of blood... paints a rather morbid picture don't you think? Could have told her to also send some blood pudding and hold the pudding... for a laugh. Just your average everyday raw steak juice, but they remember. Not your typical special order you know."

Young Vampire

"I suppose. I'll have to try it sometime..." He shudders and grimaces.

Old Vampire

"Not a bad consistency either. I'd have expected it watered down or already made into gravy. It's almost not worth the effort then the way it cakes up with lumps when you try to drink it that way." He immediately sets fangs to the plate and the blood seems to instantly disappear.

Young Vampire

"Must be alright with the way you're slurping!"

Old Vampire

"You're crazy, here have the rest."

Young Vampire

"No I don't fancy it cold... being cold blooded has its drawbacks."

Old Vampire

"Suit yourself." He continues slurping a moment longer. "Not bad," licking his lips. "So how was your own, conversion I mean? Couldn't have been half as bad as mine I'd wager?"

Young Vampire

"I guess it was natural enough or unnatural if you like, and came by way of another vampire. Probably the more typical or usual method, but for me still one reason why the presence of other vampires worries me. Like yourself I've little concern for humans and their petty annoyances. They may have caused my worst experiences but these were just circumstantial or accidental really. Vampire's on the other hand... It's so rare to meet another vampire isn't it?" Without waiting for a response, "do you think the train's on-time?"

Old Vampire

"We're not due for the last stop in Transylvania till just before dawn!"

Young Vampire

"You'd think traveling in vampire country might be a little less stressful. I'm not demanding we be catered to," he looks at his companion. "Though I don't see that as a bad thing, necessarily. It might save lives in fact... us being late!"

Old Vampire

"Yes point taken but how about that story? We have a long night yet and I imagine you'll be going all the way to the end, the very last stop? If so, you're welcome to share my carriage. I've hired a driver and there's room for two coffins of course."

Young Vampire

"Rather a novelty in these days, isn't it? A horse drawn carriage..."

Old Vampire

"Yes I suppose, but it's tradition more than anything. The horses are well-trained. They've made to trip for me many times. And the driver should make a nice meal next evening if he keeps his nerve and not desert us."

Young Vampire

"I'd think the driver'd be necessary should someone happen to spy a driverless hearse so to speak and also for crossing the rivers at least."

Old Vampire

"Funny you should mention, that is a concern of course but our way is along desolate terrain. The few people still remaining are thankfully dolts or very superstitious where it comes to vampires and driverless carriages. To show concern for the rivers tells me of your own travel experience doesn't it? Yes a curious thing about horse travel is their skittish nature when approaching moving water, just big babies when untended. More so without a bridge, but it's a problem even with a familiar route and sturdy cross way, you're right. That's why I prearrange for a driver in town, but coming from home I can drive at night. The horses won't hesitate if they feel me there with them."

Young Vampire

"You've woken in the evening to find yourself stranded by water's edge?"

Old Vampire

"No, the horses will be there you can trust in that, but yes I've been abandoned by countless drivers during daylight. I don't know what it is that gets to them. Maybe mentally, you know, I'm communicating unconsciously... dreaming most likely but I rarely have complete control until dusk and I'm awake."

Young Vampire

"Yes, that's *it* of course!"

Old Vampire

"What?"

Young Vampire

"I used to be a driver from that same town at the end of the line. Then I once drove for someone I never met, didn't even know whether there was a cargo and didn't really care. I guess I was rather a dolt in those days. I was paid a small sum by the station master when the coach was ready and told I'd receive more that night. I didn't know the destination, just told that the horses were well-trained and I need only guide them, make sure they crossed the..."

Old Vampire

"Rivers?"

Young Vampire

"Yes, the rivers."

Old Vampire

"And that evening you became a..."

Young Vampire

"Vampire!"

Old Vampire

"Ironic isn't it?"

Young Vampire

"Yes I suppose, and now after all these years... I finally meet you. I guess I can't blame you not remembering."

Old Vampire

"Sorry."

Young Vampire

"No matter I can't hold a grudge more than a few decades. But it's funny I felt a dream during that drive. If I'd been superstitious I would've turned back if the horses let me but the subject of the dream was obviously some girlfriend or female victim of yours and it so entranced me I became ensnared in its web. I could no more let loose the reins then the hopeless addict refuse his drugs. Your powers are admirable unless of course it really was a drug?" He laughs.

Old Vampire

"Interesting... by the way do you happen to remember the name of the girl in my dream?"

Young Vampire

"No sorry, I don't think it was mentioned."

Old Vampire

"Oh well... Can I expect you as my guest then?"

Young Vampire

"I guess my wounds have healed by now. Why not?"

Old Vampire

"What time do you have?"

Young Vampire

"An hour before dawn," staring out the window. "I think that's the town up ahead."

Old Vampire

"Good, my carriage will be waiting..."

I Once Was Lost

"Father, into your hands I commend his soul..."

"Son two things first, it's not 'his' soul, it's 'your' soul and technically that should be a prayer straight to God, no need for intermediaries like me though I'm flattered."

"Father this is a confession."

"Son in order to see one must first open his eyes... Of what do you confess?"

"The worst..."

"The worst sin? Son, let me tell you from experience that everyone considers their sins to be the worst unless of course they are just vain, shallow minded, weak Christians and only going through the motions of a confession. I receive my share of those believe me but I always know how to get them back on the path and started in the right direction. Your statement tells me that you are in earnest with a heavy heart so tell me then what it is you've done. Have you taken another's life?"

"Yes father, another life... I used to think that maybe it wasn't the worst sin you know, because it wasn't first... Thou shalt not kill, sixth isn't it? You must think I'm very immature don't you to think of it like that? I can't help it."

"I believe you. There have been many studies made about murderers, the way they think or what they feel about their crimes. Ironically many have been shown to think innocently, pretending nothing has happened and go on naively as a child might play a game."

"Exactly father. That's the way it used to be, as if it didn't matter... even though all the while I know it matters more than anything. But how... how do I stop? I can't."

"But you must stop. You can and you will. I'll help. I want to save you. Tell me what you've done."

"It's too late. I'm smart enough to know my soul is lost, sometimes it seems like only yesterday. I'm really very old though, very old... older than the tortoise, the redwood, the hibernating toad..."

"Enough, please no jokes. It's your sin that makes you old. Only God can lift that burden, it's much too heavy for a man to bear."

"But I am not a man. I'm an aberration, a hideous beast, a creature of the night..."

"Please don't bandy words. You are not a child. This is a very serious matter if you can indeed convince me that you are in fact a murderer, your soul is in grave peril and you can't afford to waste another moment. You must confess!"

"And what then if I can convince you? Will you be able to end my torment or ease the pain? You cannot!"

"You may very well be right, confession is not a panacea for all the soul's pain but that you even have pain should at least prove you might yet possess a soul. And isn't it presumptuous to state otherwise before you yourself are even dead? Only after death can such a determination be made and perhaps not even then as there must be a certain passage of time until the final judgment day is reached according to the book of Revelations. I'm sure you realize that! And while a confession is not a guarantee for salvation certainly only good can come of it for you."

"I suppose you're right father and I would not have come to you if I didn't believe there was some hope, but then again I would not have waited as long as I have if I thought I could convince you there were something worth saving...

106

What do you do when existence itself is a curse?"

"Please I can't take it! Tell me then how long has it been since your last confession?"

"Does that really matter?"

"Well I admit it's useful primarily in terms of the penance meted out, a gage if you will. Apparently then you are overdrawn in this account as well?"

"Yes father. Father I have killed many hundreds, thousands of people over a long period of time and while I do not claim to be the most prolific murderer of all-time I am the worst. If you will hear my confession though you will see how I had no choice but to kill physically or risk murdering their very souls as it is with me. Foreseeing such a time, inevitable time... as this I have kept a lengthy record, a journal of these crimes which I hope to recite in your presence for your Holy record... I wonder if it's fortunate it hasn't been discovered until now? So I have brought the journal with me and am prepared to read. I ask only this, will you hear my confession?"

"Yes I will..." the priest gasped holding his head in his hands.

"It may take a long time."

"Proceed my son," he whispered briefly, opening the partition to look at the darkly clad man with his large book.

"Uh-uh, bad luck isn't it?" To which the priest again closed the partition. The vampire proceeded to read from a heavy leather bound book the pages of which while protected by the large leather cover were very fragile toward the start particularly. He detailed in concise phrasing with specific dates and even times, victims who had succumbed to his attacks and died relinquishing their blood so that he might live. When possible he tried to allow that the bodies be found in circumstances that might indicate accident or suicide but otherwise did not desecrate or wantonly molest. He did not revel in the conquest of death... He also explained that only with very few exceptions had he allowed his victims enough blood that they might survive the episode to later turn vampire

107

themselves. This rarity only resulted from unexpected interruptions, bad timing or protective ornaments on the victims, usually religious trinkets or fresh garlic permitting their escape.

He talked on through the night, the murders spanning centuries of time... nobles, peasants, royalty all were his prey... farmers, merchants, herdsmen all felt his fangs... armies, business, governments none were exempt, he had laid claim to them all. As the morning hours drew near and dawn fast approached finally he finished and closed the book.

"You did well father to have such patience. I tried not to be morbid or overly descriptive, just the facts as they say on the TV police shows... And now I must go with the morning sun, but I ask you this... Is it possible that there is someone, some Christian who would have done the same?"

"I don't know the answer, I don't think anyone could answer that."

"Well then what would a Christian say if offered the choice, the choice of life or death, I've placed before you?"

"I think it is I who is faced with the choice of whether to grant absolution which in your case I'm afraid will not be easy."

"Do you not believe me? Suppose you were just given the choice, to live as a vampire... everlasting life? Isn't that your dream?" The vampire exits the booth and opens the priest's door.

"I believe that you are what you say, you needn't... ahhhh!" The vampire's canines sink deeply into the priest's neck before he can finish the sentence.

"I believe it is your nature to forgive so I'll let you live, to see... how long it may take you to change your mind, father!" The vampire places his book under the sprawled body of the near lifeless transformed priest. Going over to the baptismal he drains the holy water, knocks the large stylish wooden cross from the altar to the floor and leaves through the massive front doors to the blaring city traffic and glaring morning sunshine... and is gone.

Once upon a Midnight Dreary

The Teacher

"Let's talk about the poem. How many were frightened? Not enough it seems. Okay Aris, it was your assignment..."

Aris

"How does that old poem go? Blah, blah, blah, blah... there came a rapping, a gentle tapping at my chamber door. Something about a raven that said, 'nevermore.'"

The Teacher

"Uh and a raven with a penchant for pestering people, no more! At least we have the idea from the start that the raven won't be allowed to pester many others. So was it a highly intelligent raven seeking the company of humans or perhaps just a warm place to shelter from the outside but taking the time to learn a little English before making the attempt to move in with his hateful host? The raven once inside, only too soon realized that its irritating mannerisms and limited vocabulary incensed the man but it was too late, by then he was trapped."

Aris

"Right teacher, exactly what I was going to say."

The Teacher

"That will do Aris. Now class, is there anyone else who can tell us what this classic poem of early American literature might be saying, teaching, or even preaching for us today? Yes Todd?"

Todd

"As far as preaching, it shows the sins of one become the sins of many and vice versa. The man obviously had an aversion to wild animals, in this case birds, so the raven never had a chance even though it was so smart it could talk.

The Teacher

"Interesting Todd, but why do you mention sinning?"

Todd

"Well the guy hates birds for some reason, and likes to hurt animals which is like sinning especially if you're a conservationist. Maybe he had a bad experience, some other animal he met before already ruined it for the raven. Or he could be prejudiced about the raven being smart so now he hates all ravens because of that one..."

The Teacher

"Well thought out Todd, you've surprised me! What do you think Mary, why does the story have a talking raven?"

Mary

"To make it interesting?"

The Teacher

"Yes but why?"

Mary

"Because ravens can't really talk..."

The Teacher

"Exactly, but there's more isn't there?"

Tom

"Because it's not a raven at all!" Says a boy from the back of the class. "It probably was a Myna bird or something. They can talk and they're all black just like ravens. The guy was just stupid, he didn't know the difference..." The class laughs at his comment.

The Teacher

"Sure, that's a possibility, anyone who can hate another living thing as much as the man in the story can't be too smart can they, or can't they? But to go back to the concepts of good and evil; the bird appears to irritate him in every possible way without actually touching him. Is it a curse from hell, some form of imaginary hell he's created to punish himself for some horrible crime he's done? A talking raven can represent the guilt pangs that he knew might arrive some night. The next night it might be talking crickets or beetles..." More laughing from the class.

Mary

"Couldn't he just be working too hard and hallucinating?"

The Teacher

"Or could it be he hates someone so much, maybe a roommate or someone like Aris here..."

Aris

"Hey what'd I do now?" He starts coughing.

The Teacher

"Maybe he's planning a murder and under a lot of stress, but before that happens he focuses his anger on petty annoyances until he imagines they're growing into hideous talking ravens hounding his every move!"

Mary

"I was right!" She smiles.

Tom

"Maybe he wants to murder his wife!"

Aris

"No he's gay, you can tell! All those artsy literature dudes are." The teacher turns away from the class as if suddenly startled by the sound of their voices...

The Teacher

"I think we can safely say homophobia plays no crucial role, but there is an

111

undercurrent of violence perhaps even murder. Ask yourselves has a murder been committed? I think we all need to read it through again tonight, maybe after you've cleared you're heads spending time with your usual pursuits... sports, friends or hours of TV, and just try to imagine something you'd despise. Maybe it's something that scares you, bores you, makes you want to kill a belligerent bird. Think about it! Class dismissed."

A few stragglers lag behind the rest and come up to his desk. Before they speak he hands them extra copies of the poem to replace copies already lost from the day before. They leave, looking guilty and shrugging to each other.

The teacher stares off out the window to a grassy field where a flock of black birds hop around in a mildly agitated fashion. They are large with powerfully built beaks and appear concentrated in one central area of the flock. Suddenly something appears to have startled them as they takeoff on large expansive wings, probably the distraction of students having just been dismissed, let go early ahead of the rest.

The teacher sees there is something there in that field, several crows remain with it not willing to let it go without a fight. But someone is running closer and all the birds fly off except the largest emitting a loud caw, caw! The king crow stands on the lifeless body of a child, whose torn shirt is now ragged shreds turned red with flecks of blood extending to cover the neck and head as well. The hair is just patches of what it recently had been. The crow becomes more agitated as the running youth approaches, ducking, bobbing and weaving side to side atop the corpse. The boy now only a few steps away at last frightens off the large crow who explodes in a flurry of feathers and appears at once many times its former size. The bird circles and departs... spitting warnings as he flies. The teacher strains to hear but now there is only the sound of someone yelling for help...

A Penny for Your Soul

"Ashes to ashes, and dust to dust... he said, and that was it! They laid him to rest. Him, as if he'd been toiling all his life and deserved a rest. Or that maybe he'd been in a state of turmoil since the end and at last after days being exposed to irritating live people he'd be more comfortable with his own kind down below. But would you really be resting, I mean if you were anything at all after it all you think you'd be trying to work yourself back to the real world not enjoying some fairy tale dreamlike death? What do you think?"

"About what, vampire psychobabble?"

"Don't you ever think about it, what happens after?"

"Every time I've had one too many..."

"I guess we're old enough where it doesn't matter. I mean when they're young it's always a bad scene, such a shame... He was so youthful, had his whole life, etc.. With us it's like we can be carefree, childlike with anticipation almost, can't we? Why be paranoid about ruining an old life? How much worse can it be, the final irony, an empty insult after a life of abuse, death?"

"You're in the wrong business..."

"On the contrary. I care about the world, my surroundings, things that might affect our survival..."

"It's not worth it... you're a fanatic nerd! Or are you just hoping one time to hit the jackpot, maybe have half the town turnout, national media coverage, a country in crisis story from the inadvertent inconvenience of your latest meal?"

"And what if it happened? You wouldn't know! You'd be out at the bar tossing back shots while a rock star, or movie star, maybe even the president himself lays dead in the street a few feet away... Do you even know who he is?"

"Life is life, if you start trying to discriminate you'll just go crazy. Take yourself as a perfect example."

"Shut up, sometimes you disgust me."

"You're the one doing the talking, and don't forget you're the one going to funerals to ogle dear departeds you don't know!"

"I knew them at the end."

"I doubt it. Does a lion know the difference from a rabbit to antelope to a buffalo... hardly."

"At least with lions and tigers, they know how the herd reacts when they..."

"Go-ahead say it."

"Eat to... survive."

"Say how long has it been, was it really just a couple nights ago?"

"Why don't we try farming again? We could get a nice fat librarian this time, 'probably be so afraid we wouldn't need to tie her... nice relaxful sip snacks all night. We'd be able to rest in peace. She might last weeks!"

"You and your librarians! Relaxful, sip snacks... Food is like an addiction with you isn't it? And you're always the first to lose control, she wouldn't last the night. And what if she escaped? Just forget it."

"Remember the time we brought that dancer over, even though she didn't last..."

"Fifteen minutes?"

"She was weaker than she looked but I remember you finished drinking, and there was a movie on... anyway later before she left..."

"On my back by the way!"

"Something must happened before then, I checked... I just had a feeling. I knew she was empty, dry as a bone but I had to..."

"Could be you're an addict with an affliction of the blood or maybe you're part canine. You're probably aware how they feed."

"The point is there seemed to be more!"

"How much?"

"More than a snack?"

"But she was still..."

"Not surviving, right!"

"Maybe after all that time her vessels just had a chance to drain like small mountain streams into a lake."

"Or maybe..."

"You hoped I'd put some back? *You* should have put some back realizing yourself to be the glutton you are!"

"I didn't have to, she was like a factory I swear. For some reason she was producing it on her own even after death!"

"You know this time you might actually have something worth listening to... What is it?"

"We don't know why we need it ourselves do we, the blood? But we know we're not human. Maybe when we fed a little of ours got into hers, and caused some reaction like it does with us."

"It doesn't make more with us. That's why we have to keep drinking, isn't it!"

"Yeah but maybe there are other effects when it's outside our bodies or when it gets in a normal body?"

"There you go again. When are you going to quit talking about it and finally send away for that home chemistry set?"

"No really, we should check it out somehow."

"There's only one way to do that!"

"What?"

"We'll have to go to the cemetery and dig one up. What was the name of that last one? You probably saved the obituary."

"Better yet, I went to the funeral and saw where he is. I know that cemetery like the back of my hand."

"Well if this turns out to be something, which I strongly doubt by the way... maybe we can go after the others. We'll see how far back we can go before we detect a loss of freshness!"

"I say we give it a try. We both can't stomach anything but human blood and so far killing has been the only answer."

"Survival... before I met you I let some go occasionally. That was before, you now..."

"Yeah what happened? You never mentioned it."

"I don't know. Come on let's go, there's a moon out." (They leave their place and are en route to the cemetery.)

"What did you have to do, leave town?"

"No, well I did eventually anyway but it was just a feeling you know... that I wasn't safe, which by the way is the only real reason I let you stay with me..."

"Nice of you to say. This is probably a good time to tell you about your lost credit card..."

"But really sometimes I thought that I must've made others like us. Maybe it's just possible you know, to be tuned to these others' thoughts. There seemed to be vibes of actual... *hatred*."

"Really? You don't say? Wait, we're here so shut up. I know you're excited to be out again so soon after the last..."

"Survival mission?"

"Kill! I was going to say kill."

"Well here he is... (reading) here lies Edward Johansen, a man not sorely missed in life will be so in death..."

116

"Sounds like a threat doesn't it? Three dots and everything for effect, sort of ominous with impending doom."

"The epitaph is scary so we should turn back, is that it?"

"No just a thought I guess. I just get thoughtful in cemeteries sometimes."

"Yeah, at just a time we need to be physical. Where are the shovels?"

"Wait, look there's still a tarp down. We're in luck, they haven't filled it yet."

"Hey, let's get it off... look it's a long way down isn't it?"

"Here let me help. Look at that casket, what is that silver and polished mahogany? Why don't you jump down and open it up?"

"Why don't we both, I'm not going to haul him up for you..."

"Let's have a look." (They descend into the deep and are standing on the coffin when they hear a third voice.)

"You two amaze me!"

"What? Who's there? This isn't what it seems to be at all." (Says one from the pit.)

"Yeah and I'm not even sure what it seems to be... (Says the other from the pit.) I'm just along for the ride."

"Really, I've been hearing about the rash of unexplained deaths in the area for some time and was thinking a couple characters such as yourselves might be behind them, you know vampires... I never thought it would happen to me. But on a whim I requested in my will that my grave be kept open on the first night."

"So then your name is..."

"That's right, Edward. Edward Johansen and before you climb out of there I have a request of you two."

"What would that be?" (Suddenly a huge flood light with a brightness intensity equal that of Florida's midday summer sun shines directly down on the pair from above...)

"Please don't kill us!" (They plead cringing from the light.)

117

"Just get in the coffin and maybe I'll spare you!" Without hesitation they quickly lift the massive lid and groaning slide inside, the lid closing with a heavy thud. The third vampire then abruptly shuts off the light and instantly disappears into the grave himself to securely lock the airtight burial chamber before re-emerging from the steep hole with practiced dexterity...

"Now let's see how they like it!" He begins filling up the grave with dirt. "I bet the grave diggers don't mind a little help... this once! Oh and here's a penny for your souls..." He pauses to toss a coin into the grave which clicks noisily on the lacquered coffin then resumes his work.

First You Cry, Then You Die

Bar Girl

"He made me cry, officer. He, he... abused me!"

Officer

"How did he abuse you miss?"

Bar Girl

"Well first he bought me drinks. We were at the Red Parrot, you know the bar and..."

Officer

"Then he bought *you*?"

Bar Girl

"Now you're abusing me!"

Officer

"Sorry, just the way you're dressed, it's kind of suggestive."

Bar Girl

"If you must know, I do work for the place but that's no reason. He had no right to..."

Officer

"To what?"

Bar Girl

"Oh forget it! Cops are never around when you need 'em, then when they're there it's like *you're* that criminal... Why is that?"

Officer

"Are you a criminal miss?"

Bar Girl

"Oh, just forget it will you?"

Officer

"Sure ma'am, sure you're alright then? (She nods.) Alright then."

Partner

"What was that about?" (Says to cop getting in the patrol car.)

Officer

"Someone made her cry or something. She may be afraid to talk about it."

Partner

"She sounds like a user... looks like one too. Maybe we should bring her in on substance abuse."

Officer

"She said she was abused. Maybe we should bring her in for her own safety?"

Partner

"You can't keep 'em safe from themselves though, and if we arrested everyone who needed that kind of protection we'd have to cordon off the city."

Officer

"She was afraid. (He starts to the engine.) Her type doesn't usually call the cops."

Partner

"I know what you mean, users. They're all alike. They know they need help but too afraid to turn themselves in!"

Officer

"No, no. (Just then they hear a scream. They stop the car and run over to the scene, a girl - provocatively dressed, laying limp on the sidewalk.) That's her... apparently she was right to call us."

Partner

"You're right, she's dead. Probably an overdose."

Officer

"Why would she scream... Look and her cheeks are still wet from crying, eyes bloodshot. I'll call it in."

Partner

"I'll look for paraphernalia... (turning her head) Looks like ah fresh needle tracks in her neck, how disgusting!"

Officer

"Do you have enough for the report yet? (He says trying not to look.) C'mon it's kind of cold, let's wait in the car."

Partner

"Yeah, I guess. No needles... her boyfriend must have shot her up right after we left."

Officer

"This isn't good. (They get in the car.) We were the last to see her alive. It's after hours, no one around and just minutes after an official call... I even checked the mirror. She was standing there alone one minute, and dead the next with us only yards away. Maddening isn't it?"

Partner

"Pushers are bold these days."

Officer

"I don't think bold is the word. Here's the ambulance. Hey guys I don't think your gear will help much with this one, might want to let the coroner have her..."

Medic

"Where is she?"

Officer

"Right over... What the heck?"

Partner

"Don't tell me!"

Officer

"She's gone!"

Medic

"Happens a lot, you'd be surprised. The ones that seem to be the worst will get up and walk away before we can get to 'em! ...Sure lots of times. Why don't you circle the block a couple times, she might still be in the area. We'll follow you."

Officer

"Sure, sorry about this. First time for us! (They drive around a little while but there's no sign of the victim. They wave to the departing ambulance.) This is unbelievable. I know dead and that girl was dead! We've got a sick corpse stealing murderer on our hands!"

Partner

"Either that or an addict on some very heady stuff and, my guess is X or Z, maybe crank or even Dupont, you know huffing. Very nasty..."

Officer

"I suppose we ought to hold off on the report, or perhaps make it a routine disturbance call with possible injuries..."

Partner

"Right by me."

In the ensuing weeks many similar incidents are known to occur though many cases go unreported. Bodies are resurrected often before ambulance crews arrive or somehow disappear mysteriously from hospital emergency rooms and morgues soon after regaining consciousness. The authorities are baffled and can only hope that some evil-minded genius soon comes forward with an explanation as might be expected in serial cartoon dramas like

'Batman' or 'Superman.' 'Spiderman?' None is forthcoming.

One common or central theme seeming to unite the crimes is the obvious evidence of the victims crying or having cried shortly before death. Police reason that this may indicate emotional attachment to or manipulation by the killer, hypnosis or yes, even a drug influence of some type. Even more vexing than the elusive killer is the fact that the victims themselves remain at-large, perhaps hiding or taking part in the bizarre crime spree as well.

Then as if by magic, divine intervention or the like, one is discovered... A body that had died, been resurrected, disappeared, then apparently died again had been found. But similar to the Roswell aliens, (or the crashed UFO that yielded dead aliens now stored deep underground in Roswell, New Mexico) there is so much secrecy surrounding the find that the body is again lost along with data that may have provided needed clues. The body though is rumored to have been very old or withered in appearance while at the same time it showed some indications of having been recently much younger. Notably the condition and style of clothes, good bone and teeth structure, and the presence of a newly purchased wooden stake through the heart all indicated a recent demise.

Anyway the big break in the case, as they say in detective lingo, occurred when a funeral parlor worker placed one of their recently deceased client's bodies, a crime victim, into one of their premier mirrored caskets. This top-of-the-line model had a completely mirrored inner surface for added vanity after death. But in so doing so the worker noticed this had a striking effect on the corpse... it completely vanished before the attendant's eyes. Retrieval from within brought it once more to its real deathly state but now identified as definitely suspicious, the corpse could be watched by professionals. The surveillance was stepped up much more that night and late that evening the body, sure enough, resumed the functions of living and was followed to the municipal cemetery... where the police were shocked to observe the comings and goings of well, ghosts. What else could they be?

At this point the 'case' or 'cases' became even more shrouded in secrecy as high-tech security in the form of special fencing, alarms and cameras were added around the cemetery. This however only seemed to have the effect of protecting the cemetery's 'ghost' residents from investigators and the curious public. For some reason film records of ghost activity was of unacceptable quality in helping provide identification or accurate detail of the apparitions. The only preventive measure that had any positive benefit was the exhumation of the recently deceased during the light of day. This caused the curious withering or drying phenomenon which then appeared to represent true death.

Unfortunately the nocturnal lethal activity continued and rather than endlessly conduct the morbid examinations it was decided that officers go undercover in an attempt to act as bait and draw out the malevolent force behind these insidious and murderous assaults...

Officer

"Okay everyone check your radios. Being properly miked is what's crucial to this operation."

Partner

"Correction, the bait, er girl, uh excuse me, female officer is more crucial of course... We're just backup, because we were able to get close to the perp that first night. Or one of us did... (The partners glare at each other.)

Female Officer

"Talk around the station is that the chief still blames you guys for that bar girl's death. Hopefully you'll have a chance to redeem yourselves saving my life... I'm game if you are."

Officer

"Sure game, prey, bait... easy for you to say."

Female Officer

"What?"

Partner

"It's about time we got this drug sucking slime off the street."

Female Officer

"I'd heard there was no evidence of drug involvement..."

Officer

"Never mind him, he came from a drug environment... just watch yourself out there. This nut might be just working some deep emotional mind trip... All we do know is that he likes to make them cry. That's our only solid clue."

Partner

"That and the fact we've seen how he punctures the neck to get his pus filled poisons to work in the blink of an eye."

Female Officer

"What?"

Officer

"He takes some getting used to. (He glances sideways as partner.) Listen, don't be alarmed, we just noticed some unusual neck markings on the first victim is all. They seem to go away after death though, especially since other incidences haven't been reported yet."

Female Officer

"Oh, that's comforting, that the marks aren't there when I'm dead. Are you two going to be there when I'm... attacked?"

Officer

"Sure we will... wouldn't miss it! Well we better get started. We'll be just around a corner listening in."

Partner

"Cover your neck!" (He says as she's leaving. She leaves walking down the sidewalk not looking back.)

Officer

"Hey I have a thought, it may be just sheer physical pain that causes the lacrimation, the tearing. Maybe from a bite on the neck! Too late to tell her now, she may have her volume up, we don't want to spook the perp."

Partner

"Drugs cause your internal pain... take your PCP, your smack, your crack. Those names aren't pretty for a reason!"

Officer

"Alright, let's listen... Is yours working? I'm getting static."

Female Officer

"Oh hello there." (She says to a man in a long black cape and formal wear.)

Man in Cape

"Good evening. Awful late to be out alone isn't it?" (He looks into her eyes.)

Female Officer

"Yes, I'm glad I ran into you, a nice gentleman. I just left my friends. We were talking about the strange murders and what's happened at the cemetery..."

Man in Cape

"Yes, most strange."

Female Officer

"They say he makes his victims cry first. Why do you suppose that is? Maybe he makes them plead for their lives..."

Man in Cape

"I'd say it's a combination of things. There's one thing in life he's perfected, his murders are his art. You can't blame the artist his appreciation. Only at the highest levels can an artist elicit such a response... Don't you agree? (He bores his gaze deeply into hers...) Won't you cry for me? (He clamps his jaws tightly around her trembling neck as a tear trickles down her face.)

Female Officer

"Fellows, now would be a good time!" (She whispers.)

A Little Respect For The Lady

The clang of hardened steel resonated through the forest's clear crisp air. She'd seen it before as one combatant lay dying the victor raised his long sword and plunged it through his opponent's heart. She watched his blood ebb away. The hamlet's male population had decimated itself on her behalf. This time the squabble had resulted over the mere tone one of the young men had used in addressing her... and in all the excitement of the battle she couldn't remember now which one of the two it had been or whether his tone was objectionable. The point was that it had been objected to and vigorously. The winner was now bowing ceremoniously to her and she returned his attention with a smile. He bowed again allowing her to be on her way... What would it be next time she wondered, maybe the way they looked at her or what clothes she chose to wear? This was a definite possibility she decided and at this rate it was certain she'd be declared a witch if there wasn't some way to stop the needless carnage. Taking a lover at her young age would only spell her doom though and hasten the witch calling process so it would have to be something else but something dramatic.

She felt cursed to have been born in this era, hers was a beauty born too soon. She should eat and grow herself into oblivion to stop the madness, the competition for her hand. But that would give the others of the town, the women or the older folk more reason to hate her for consuming the limited resources. Perhaps she might find some poison plant to turn herself ugly and undesirable but she couldn't see harming herself purposely on account of people who seemed only so many roguish oafs and simpletons most of the time. And then she really would be a witch wouldn't she? At least if she were eventually branded a witch, in these times witches were held in awe for their powers and even revered with esteem for their knowledge of the healing arts. Of course she realized she had no powers or knowledge of healing so she could only become a bad witch and then probably be forced from the town when the truth was finally known. She knew no other home but the town and had never traveled. She thought if she were to meet a witch maybe she could learn enough to become a good witch but the town had had no witches... ever as far a she knew. The only news they had of them had come from distant travelers just passing through. She wondered if she might leave someday in the company of one of these infrequent visitors. If they weren't swift enough, it was sure the party'd be hunted down and killed so that she might be returned to a proper suitor. She seemed to be having the dreams more often lately as these strange acts of violence and death played out around her in real life.

What bothered her most was the jealousy of the other women. How many now would be without families of their own due to this insane violent competition for attention which had torn apart the young male population in such a short time while she was still several years from the eligible age to marry. She was sure many had already secretly plotted her death... Her parents could give her no counsel but to stay home and wear only plain clothes but all the styles of clothes of the town were quite plain anyway. They were a town of simple farmers, hunters and builders of shelters. The few nicer garments that did exist usually became stolen and found their way to her doorstep as gifts which she'd then have to puzzle over and return to their rightful owners. Schooling and church going were not strict requirements and didn't hold regular daily sessions but if she were not seen for weeks then violence would erupt and be even worse than what it would otherwise be. Soon she would have finished with school, in just only less than a year but she knew it was expected she make herself available to be seen regularly in town or at church or things would get worse... And she'd hear the reports of it from other family members on their return from town or church services.

The carnage was terrible, sometimes three or four on a single day, always fighting to the death. She couldn't believe she was the cause but then people would tell that they died with her name on their lips. She'd heard stories that men went to war and fought bravely because of their loves but to go to battle because of the object of their affection was only madness to her. She hated them all for it but didn't want to let them know. They didn't deserve to know her feelings, just let them die. If they were stupid enough to keep killing each other...

Then one day in a rare showing of frivolity and goodwill the hamlet was holding a fair where organized competitions might be watched and applauded. Before the games it was announced that anyone caught intentionally inflicting serious injury or death would themselves be killed or banished and only dull unsharpened weapons were allowed to be used in combat. Had they at last come to their senses she hoped? Young men might relieve their aggression in a harmless fashion, if that is, there were anyone left who might be so inclined. She supposed there were those still left since in order for someone to be killed fighting, there must be someone to have wielded the killing blows. Could the same man have accomplished all the killing himself? She didn't know and couldn't bear to consider it... if so he certainly hadn't come to her announcing the fact. No, she would have recollected a telling a fact as that. In the battles she'd witnessed, they'd been different at least.

The events preceded at a leisurely pace as she watched from the stands with her family. She was surprised there were really as many able bodied men left as presented themselves but it was apparent most were the older more

129

mature men of the town, already married and passed the prime of life. There was a notable void of slender brash youths ready to throw caution to the wind against stronger opponents. They had been previously eliminated from life with their own cryptic blood sports... As there were just a few protective armor suits available only one or two competitions occurred at a time. There was jousting, the mace and sword hand to hand matches, crossbow marksmen, and hammer tossing as well... In the matches contestants were directed not to try for vital areas intentionally and only minor injuries were inflicted as a result.

By late afternoon she grew fatigued. She really did not want to be there. She had seen her fill of such contests in recent months and her parents and others nearby kept watchful eyes on her to be sure she would not get caught up in more of the violence rumored to happen so often in her presence... She was not used to being out in the sun this length of time. She was pale and quite frail from all the worry and constant attention she'd received. Her mother recently had been keeping a close watch over her at home, not permitting her to work in the fields where she reasoned someone might make an attempt to kill or rape the girl even if just to end the madness. She felt herself perspiring heavily... then just as suddenly it stopped, feeling her extremities grow colder. She fainted and didn't awaken until several hours later when she was back home having recovered from the sunstroke. When she came to she asked if there had been anymore bloodshed and if anyone she knew had been hurt... fortunately not, she was told. And her father and brothers had performed admirably in their respective events. But she was not reassured.

She was restless that night and unable to sleep. She waited for the terrible news from a messenger she somehow knew would come. Later the next morning a messenger did come telling of a horrible scene of bloodshed and degradation occurring after the fair had ended and the audience departed. It seems some of the younger lads of the village hadn't been permitted to participate probably due to the fears they may be involved in the killings or be at risk themselves. They had dared each other and gone to the tent where the weapons and armor now readily available lay in open exhibit for their appreciative glances and private inspection... What happened next could hardly have been anticipated except in some enchanted, bewitched or otherwise unearthly realm. Her name was mentioned and they each took pains to describe her unnatural beauty but that she fainted made her seem to them a princess under a powerful spell. They debated the lengths they would go to break the spell. Then one of them said they had missed their chance and that she would remain enchanted forever because they were cowards that day and didn't fight.

"You can probably guess what next unfolded..." The messenger relayed the grizzly news to her family and herself. The entire group now lay bloodied and dead. Only one of them survived their ordeal and is now the only young man left in the entire hamlet except for her brothers. And they've probably only been spared the strange combats as they pose no threat to his vulnerability, a romance with her. The messenger pointed to the girl who cringed with anxiety and confused revulsion. "It is unbelievable yet undeniably true that this one man or boy wanting to act a man is the cause of so much death and despair. He must be a kind of master of disguise himself not have been so identified until now but this he told to me and admitted as much. And he does not even live in the hamlet itself but in the forest to the north. Though he has the appearance of a boy he talks as one much older and made this request of me that I come to you and beg you to go to him freely so that he might at last control these terrible urges."

She and her family sat in mute shocked silence until finally her mother voiced her stern and haughty rejection, quickly affirmed by the others and herself as well. Her mother then insisted that this be only a fanciful tale of some absurd imaginings, for how could a boy come and go and not be known and live by himself in the woods? The messenger could only say the killings are indeed not a light matter and were they not so real, he might agree that the boy's request appears absurd. "He comes to town only to see her, the object of his desires and drink the blood of his rivals. He lives a hunting life needing little more than his skill affords him but please... I believe him to be serious on my word. The entire town itself may be in danger!" They sat again in stunned silence, the messenger's words almost deafening to their ears. Her mother turned her back to him and would not look around until she was sure he'd left.

Hunting parties were sent out to search the north woods but no avail... She knew she couldn't let her mother keep her prisoner forever. She'd heard the legends about vampires and their powers, still she wasn't sure she believed. One day though, probably soon there would be more blood and then it would be on her hands and the whole town would know... She had no choice. She would go to the forest and find him or he would find her. If he turned out to be a kind of magical beast then she would die as the others. But If he was only a boy thirsty for blood she'd make him show a little respect for her, nearly a lady, somehow. Though she may be just a pretty girl, if she were old enough to love then he must be old enough to be killed... and there were many sharp stakes in the forest.

Everything's Glazed Over

"The first wave may only last a few months though residual primary effects on earth could be measured in years if there aren't any secondary waves. They're predicting significant recovery may begin in five or ten years..."

"Outer space radiation... Unbelievable! Right out of a '50s comic book."

"Well we've known of its presence for quite a while. The Hubble picked it up as a zone of fast moving isotopes entering the edges of the galaxy years ago but they weren't predicting us seeing actual radiation storms for thousands of years, five thousand to be exact..."

"A few weeks is what they're saying now is that it?"

"Yeah but it's better than no warning at all."

"That's debatable... a few weeks to prepare for nuclear winter. What are we supposed to do build a fallout shelter in a few weeks?"

"It shouldn't be nearly as bad as a nuclear winter scenario. After all, this stuff has been traveling through space a long time, lots of time for dispersion, radioactive decay, etc.."

"What caused it anyway, the big bang?"

"Doubtful, radioactive decay would have taken the punch out of that stuff billions of years ago. Maybe just a collapsing black hole or cosmic wind from a new galaxy... Most likely a supernova, some star exploding and sending its unspent fuel hurdling through space at tremendous velocities."

"Hey maybe like that star they saw you know, when Jesus was born couple thousand years ago?"

"Possible I guess. Radioactive half-lives for heavy isotopes can last 10,000 years... the radioactive ions would naturally travel much slower than the photons, or the light from the explosion."

"Naturally, but does two thousand years buy us enough time?"

"Depends on what kind of star it was..."

"Worst case scenario then is life as we know it ceases, and an ice age starts that lasts a million years?"

"You've been doing a little outside reading I take it?"

"Magazines, nothing too heavy. C'mon give it to me straight. I may not be able to deal with it but if you know something you've got to tell me. Everyone in the department knows you're the only one who really earned his degree."

"Thanks I guess... What they're projecting is five to ten thousand before total cool down, what I said before. I don't have inside information. It's not like at the racetrack."

"Oh... if you say so Carmen."

"Well if you really want my opinion, I'd say there's a good chance a sizable amount of plant life will be affected even in a short period of time like a few months. Then it follows they'll be a die off in the rest of the food chain. Fewer vegetarian animals will mean fewer carnivores. With less plants they'll be an inverse greenhouse effect resulting in colder weather and further die offs..."

"Sounds like those dinosaur extinction theories, including ice ages."

"They've been well substantiated in the geological record."

"Great, but what about us, human people, specifically? I'm thinking a lot of cancer long term?"

"Increased exposure to various types of radiation has been causative and curative as well. It's main effect is on rapidly dividing cells such as seen in cancer and in the skin. Ironic, isn't it that cells most susceptible to the sun's ultra violet rays would be found in the skin, those most easily accessible?"

"I see, stay undercover. And try to find some new black friends? What else?"

"The digestive and respiratory tracks also contain cells with a high turnover rate."

"I get it, eating and breathing are out. So that about covers it?"

"If we can live on previously processed food, which may be necessary anyway due to die off, and utilize air filters and purifiers we might do alright. We'll probably only experience a weakening of the immune systems and some slight chromosome damage, similar to heavy marijuana abuse."

"I feel better already thanks."

"Oh, also you might want to save a sample of your bone marrow, just in case for reinjection later if you lose all ability to produce immune cells or blood... which sometimes occurs in radiation therapy you know."

"That much I know. I haven't been a blood scientist all these years to miss out on a chance to donate bone marrow to myself. God, what a world..."

"Just a reminder. By the way, it's more professional to actually say 'hematological' once in a while, *blood's* so morbid... As far as marrow, the more samples the better. Imagine being toxic with a poison that'll still be active in 10,000 years... That's a lot of transplants!"

"Yes, I'll try to remember. I think I could go for a donut. Maybe I'll bring a box of them to the guys over in Aging Research. I'll remind them about the marrow donations and see what they've been working on..."

"Good idea. Now's a good time to try a new drug isn't it?"

"Hey it's the blood guy, cover your necks!"

"Hi, how are things with you fellows, sorry to interrupt... everyone knows you're doing the most indispensable work."

"Yeah, that's why our funding always gets cut first."

"I don't think I've ever been paid. So what do you think about the radiation storm..."

"Well everyone here thinks it's a scourge from God because of what we're working on... otherwise we're planning to come to work like always except wearing the standard radiation hazard suit and possibly an extra seven layers of clothes underneath. What about you?"

"God, I haven't even thought about coming to work. I was only trying to decide the best place to hide. Hey by the way Carmen says it's a good idea to try and donate some marrow just in case you know..."

"Things go to hell in a hand basket? Thanks, we know the drill. Say are these donuts for us?"

"Sure, I'm no teaser."

"God, good ol' Carmen. How could he not be a blood man? I bet he names his kids after the clotting factors, doesn't he?"

"Good one... I don't think he's got time for kids."

"Of course, how stupid of me... so what brings you over to see us heretics besides the latest global disaster?"

"Oh, just wondering you know... what you have to get us through this, anything?"

"It's probably the most unnatural natural disaster ever, huh? Yeah, well this is usually only top secret grant review information but for a box of donuts I can tell you... that we've been working on a combination or distillation of growth hormone releasing factor, erythrocyte free blood and yogurt farmers of the Himalayas... No really, we think we might have something with the bloodless blood."

"Hmmm. That the sounds new. How would you transport nutrients and gases?"

"Well in all seriousness we don't know how it works yet. But some strange species of Amazon bat, Diphylla ecaudata, has blood that works on the principle. A jungle farmer discovered it. 'Said he was bitten and afterward never felt better. A sample of his blood demonstrated the same effect... all the RBC's had hemolyzed yet the blood still functioned to amazing effect. It also caused the same reaction in our test animals and aside from some anemia and sun sensitivity symptoms they behaved normally. Of course we also monitored for some known diseases like rabies, and malaria, even sleeping sickness, but the critters are all normal. Well perhaps a bit aggressive... Otherwise they're much better than normal."

"How so?"

"Their other cells have all seemed to stop replicating. At first we thought it was a severe toxicity to some unknown hemolyzing poison but they haven't died and all the tests have shown none of their cells are dividing."

"Even the skin?"

"Yeah and what's more there doesn't appear to be any need for them to divide. In fact they don't appear to be functioning at all. Why would a cell divide if it didn't need to function?"

"I don't understand, they're not dead?"

"For instance, the basal layer of dermis, where new skin cells are formed has fused into a tough fibrous band and the other skin cells just remain and are never sloughed off. We've tagged cells and observed them still intact and in place after several generations of cells should have come and gone. A curious thing though, after the animal feeds this basal layer reappears briefly... almost like a computer doing a system's check."

"What do you make of it?"

"We guess it's something to do with the blood, some property causing both the cessation and prolongation of life..."

"Now you're starting to talk like Carmen."

"God forbid! Anyway we've isolated an unknown agent we believe may be responsible."

"You think it might protect against radiation?"

"Probably, we've tried other stimuli to induce mitosis with no effect as long as there is enough blood."

"Wait a minute, what do you mean?"

"Well as I've said there's some property, an unknown agent at work in the blood fluid and by some process maybe simple dehydration, the levels of this unknown factor drop and then they have to be replenished. Interestingly a meal consisting of blood itself seems to be the only highly efficient method to accomplish this."

"Any blood?"

"I suppose, if it has cells, especially and what blood doesn't except well, the host. I'm sure you get the picture..."

"But you haven't tested it on humans? You think I could get a sample to show Carmen?"

"Protocols don't permit it..."

"I know... at this juncture. You sound like you're running for president, I just hope protocols can stop x-rays too..."

"Yeah, ha! Maybe things will change due to the space invasion! I don't see the harm in letting you see a small sample... Here, why not take a baby bat, and observe the effects yourself? Keep him in his cage though. He likes plates of blood, lots of them."

"Oh, okay. Thanks guys."

"Sure. Maybe you blood guys can find out how our missing link works!"

"We'll give it a try. Hey you sure he's okay? He looks dead and his eyes are all glazed over."

"That's normal for him, he won't wake-up usually during the day..."

"Hmmph. That's probably what I'll be like after the radiation storm. Can you imagine, maybe another ice age? And everything'll be glazed over? You sure he isn't dead? He even feels cold. Ouch, he bit me!"

The Hideous One

There was a story once about someone who cast such a hideous reflection, she'd been immortalized as 'an apparition to haunt the corridors of time.' The moral of the story was that she'd been evil and her evilness had shown through eventually to expose her. I remember I had laughed out loud when I'd come to that part because I was also ugly, so much so I hadn't used a mirror in years. I was evil as well... but I was glad this story had been about a woman, in truth only nonsense made up to show how people became prejudiced about things, things like being bug ugly! The book was in the fiction department anyway making it an easy bet the story was... untrue. I couldn't have cared, though I felt relieved just to be able to read it. After all, we all have our sickness don't we? So then someone has to be the sickest. It's only natural but reading about things similar to what I've done was well, awkward at first.

Being extremely unattractive is not an excuse for my actions rather just a cloak of convenience. You might be born to play basketball if you're tall or ride race horses if you're not. For me, it's the wildlife... In the story the woman, let's call her Hag, had been harassed and beaten early on, abused so relentlessly she finally snapped, going off for long walks in the park and scaring little children and their pets, making the flesh of others crawl with revulsion.

"Hello child," she'd say. "Try this nice sour ball. If you suck it real hard your eyes will pop out!" She'd laugh and drop a sour ball and yell, "oh there it goes!"

The children watched horrified while the youngest kids picked up candies and attempted to eat them. When the parents came over to give her a spiteful look they'd be sent reeling seeing her close-up. "I was just trying to feed the birds wasn't I?" She'd say. "And they got in the way!"

A mother would shout, "you don't feed birds candy!"

"I can feed them whatever I want, can't I?" The Hag'd say. Sometimes if they didn't leave quickly enough she'd throw the candy which stung like small stones and continue on her way. She'd also been known to spit on children who came too close to her house and to kick stray dogs. Garbage men picking up the trash in the early morning reported to their fellows they'd seen rats poking their heads from the attic vent fins for a little healthy fresh air and sunshine. And occasionally they'd been in the trash as well scurrying quickly to avoid the jaws of death waiting inside the truck.

Her neighbors sometimes complained to the county commission about her high bushes that were more like tall thickly bunched trees and the heavily vined fencing that kept all but the hardiest busybodies from peering into her backyard. The ones that had seen her herself though resigned themselves to having to see her as little as possible.

There was also the issue of unusual noises and smells which she explained as being due to her pets and chimney fires, hopefully not in combination. Investigators sent letters but were reluctant to visit after meeting her once, on their initial appointment.

Most vexing of course were that area children had gone missing but few were willing to accept that some horrid cranky woman was absconding with children to feed them to her pets (the rats?), or roast them over a nice chimney fire for dinner.

For me however it was only too easy to guess the obvious. The Hag was a hoarder, one of a special type vampire as there exist rare blood types among humans. Hoarders for some bizarre technical reason cannot digest adult human or animal blood in the normal way... we must subsist almost entirely on blood cooked to a boil then simmered slowly to congeal the proteins, 'denaturing' the scientists call it. Unlike most vampires who readily absorb raw blood and derive complete sustenance from it, hoarders are one of a type who suffer violent reactions, massive painful scarring and dramatic psychic episodes when forced to drink it in its pure liquid form. The effect is rather similar to being subjected to severe physical abuse say pummeling, with no recourse but to seek out the blood of young children or resort to immature animals whose blood properties are more manageable and easy to digest, especially when cooked.

I suddenly realized then when almost toward the end of the story, the hag was real or at least based on someone so similarly afflicted... I had heard there'd been others, that we'd been labeled 'hoarders' due to our bizarre eccentric habits... collecting things that children particularly might enjoy, or might put them at ease and better attract them. That had been so long ago though, I'd almost forgotten there may be others. The obstacle of our frightening appearance and the inability to overcome it as a normal vampire might easily do proved too much for them I imagine.

'Hoarders,' like vampires, can live at the periphery of human existence... coaxing, taunting, tricking unwittingly victims into a bit of apoplectic blood sucking. The one difference however being that the meal must be regurgitated for proper preparation later and if withheld too long from doing so something more an animal in mind and body are the inevitable results...

So I didn't start out wanting to kill, least of all the youngest and most innocent just for my daily bread as the expression goes. I'm sure Hilda didn't either. I decided to change her name again to Hilda, shortened from the original -- Broomhilda, and certainly more appropriate than *Hag* considering her disability. It just comes natural to a hoarder, which again may be another reason for our lack of numbers. A litany of death in your wake has a tendency to produce outrage, suspicion and yes, even capture. But I'm careful, only not so careful as to not kill of course. Being a normal vampire helps a lot since as we all know evidence is destroyed in death, wounds healed in the immortal state and even bodies themselves vanish after a time if unattended to exist as 'undead' themselves. But our lot is not that easy. A 'hoarder' has no such effect on his victim, the wounds we inflict in death remain intact, unchanged, damning. And our lack of procreation then the final insult, the reason for our few numbers... a kind of impotence I guess.

Suddenly I was tapped on the shoulder by the librarian I suppose it was but I'd turned with such a snarl she'd practically flown behind the nearest stack of books... I'd been dreaming again at the library when I should be home watching those kids. I'd had them several weeks already and it wouldn't do if they were to become bored and actually risk injury or death in an attempt to 'runaway.' No, they would die another way, I was certain of it and besides there was far too much there to hold their interests, to entertain them among the things I'd collected these many years... things I know children like.

As I left the library and passed a large mirror positioned in the foyer near the entranceway I looked at the intricate gold leaf design of the frame and laughed. Mirrors don't bother me. Imagine being captured by a mirror... It was absurd to even think about it!

The Afterlife Shows Promise But You're Death Needs Work

The afterlife, the afterlife, the afterlife... I know it well yet haven't died. Vampires, the undead, creatures of the night are with me constantly, every waking moment, every shard of dream explains their curse to me... that I am one with them. I know the voices must be insane, that I am insane but what can I do? Suicide is not an option for a vampire unless of course you know what you're doing. And I detest violence in all its forms yet they don't call it 'madness' for nothing!

I don't know what to do, I wait and wait but the voices are always there, always there. Though I have remembrances of my former life, and a nine to five job... holding the pickles and the lettuce! But they say it's the postal jobs that lead to insanity. What do 'they' know anyway... I've never had any problems with my mail but try getting something done 'your way' anywhere, at just about any kind of business whose motto has something to do with 'service being first' and you'll find the first law of physics, that all things tend toward disorder, is what is really first. So this is what I've been reduced to... talking to myself about physics and searching for a low rent preferably basement apartment. I don't even need an actual address, who needs mail in the afterlife?

The voices tell me to surrender and with open arms embrace the charms of

143

the night. I want to fly blind raving mad into the icy darkness of my soul to find the voices that I may ask them when and how it all happened. And why did it happen to me, the craving, the endless craving for blood! Was I the subject of a medical experiment, a victim of attack by bat, wolf or vampire? If so, why should I be able to walk down a street and pass right by whomever had been responsible without hope of recognition. I ask you? You must tell me, you must! And why do I keep talking to myself?

I don't want to watch my new friends, passing acquaintances, store clerks and neighbors grow old and whither at my feet... and what of my family, would they know me now? It seems such a longtime has passed before I had even thought of them... how could that be so? I like to think of that song 'Say, Say, Say' and the part that goes, 'Take, Take, Take what you need but don't leave me here forever!' How sad to have been left all alone, frightfully alone in the afterlife forever. I want to scream out a name, hold its shape in my pocket and watch as I burst into flames with the new dawn.

I am hopelessly insane. I know that now. But I want to stay at this place, a new place I have found that offers some peace and a little tranquility from the world, from a world of sharpened fangs and torn throats, horrible power and cruel invincibility... and from death. The ground is warm and soft, the soil like fine powder and sweet from someone's constant loving care and attention. At long last I feel I could rest here deep within the earth and possibly a casket. I can detect there is a nice casket at just this spot, my mind is able to probe this place and it will do for me...

"Sir I'm going to have to ask you to leave now."

"What?" The vampire looks around startled.

"Well, the funeral service ended hours ago and the cemetery closes at night. I'm sure you understand."

"Well, I guess... No, no I definitely don't understand! Who are you anyway?"

"I'm the grounds keeper, you know, landscaping, pit digging, pit filler upper... that kind of thing. Oh, and I'm also in charge of closing up, sorry."

"Do you know who I am?"

"Well, I'd probably guess you're a mourner for the Johnson grave since that's where you've been kneeling for the past hour or so... not that I've been watching you or anything."

"The Johnson grave? Do I look like a Johnson family member?"

"No, I really wouldn't know sir. The funeral was a while ago and I don't remember faces to well. Weren't you at the burial?"

"Yes, of course. You don't think I'd come just for the scenery do you? That'd be crazy wouldn't it? Do you think me mad?"

"Please sir stay back I didn't mean anything by it! Ahhhh!"

"So much for dining out tonight. Yes, this would make a very nice home indeed. Of course *you'll* have to find your own place and we'll have to see about another site for Mr. Johnson as well... I'm beginning to feel better already."

"I'll get you sometime, I swear!" The grave digger coughed.

"You? I thought you were, excuse the expression, six feet under... I dined too quickly I suppose. Here, let me finish the job, no wait! If you 'crossover' with that grudge you could be cross forever... Well this may not work but let's try." The vampire approaches the dying man again and this time places his hands at the man's head and says, "Forget! I want you to forget everything, everything that is except landscaping. You're very good at landscaping. The graves are very beautiful... You've changed my whole outlook. I like it. I want you to stay on later and continue. Consider it, will you?" He lets the man's head fall to earth as he breathes his last.

"Either way it makes no difference. I've been thinking of cashing in. There doesn't seem to be a lot of call for my abilities in the afterlife. I'm mad you see as you soon will be. You've known what it's like to live among the dead, tending their needs. Now you'll be able to live among the living as the undead, you'll see. We are the true misfits of the world, you and I."

Damned If You Even Think about It

"She was a foul moron possessed of a blackness that exuded ennui..." he said. "There were many who loathed her, hated her but above all else wanted her death."

"Did you know her that well master?" Redveldt replied, continuing their game.

"No... but I think it helps to make up reasons sometimes when a death is inevitable."

"Very eccentric of you, master. Anyway she was alone walking in the red light district. She offered no resistance. I don't think there'll be any problems."

"Good Redveldt."

"She seemed quite impressed when I told her I was a doctor, probably because of how much more I might pay... and I was impressed too that she believed me. Maybe there's hope for me yet?"

"Let's not be too excited but you're beginning to see aren't you? Life is tenuous at best, isn't it? An accidental laceration, just one severed major vessel say in the neck... is enough to stop the works. The precious bodily fluids are so easily lost. A shaving mishap, eh Redveldt?"

"What master?"

"Come, let's prepare for the operation."

"I know what you're really thinking master."

"What?" The Count stood over her, staring at his handy work.

"Sex!"

"You're crazy Redveldt, I'm no necrophiliac!"

"You mean you never thought about it, never even consider it? You gotta admit they're beautiful sometimes, the way they just lay there you know, listless like that. As if to say..."

"Will you shut up?"

"Well I don't know how you can resist, and it's safer too."

"I've heard about doctors like you, Redveldt."

"Just watch the machines and keep your hands off until I say so. What do you mean safer?"

"Whatever diseases she's got are dying with her aren't they? Heck she's probably AIDS free by now, if she had it unless it's contaminated the blood... it is a disease of the blood though isn't it?"

"Please Redveldt!"

"I've got to hand it to you master, performing complicated procedures from just reading books and having a high school education. It shows you what money and determination can do."

"And please Redveldt call me 'Count'... You can save any compliments till after. Being a doctor, you should know that there's plenty of bugs in a carcass, if anything she's more diseased."

"Those are your death bugs, from the necrosis. The others, your conventional disease bugs are already gone I'd bet."

"If you say so."

"Sure and your necrosis hasn't really started yet so now's the best time isn't it?"

"For what, sex?"

"She is a looker, Count *master.*"

"What, don't I pay enough that you have to talk like that in the middle of a delicate procedure? Scoop up some of the excess blood and don't throw it out."

"We are criminals aren't we, so why not a little fun? If we're caught at least we'll have better memories for the long prison nights..."

"You're disgusting Redveldt."

"It's my criminal mentality coming through I guess."

"I'd have hated to be your partner in cadaver class!"

"Oh master, what do you call the only course in medicine were you fail if your patient survives?"

"The cadaver classes?"

"Good old Med school humor."

"Focus Redveldt."

"Let me hear again why you despised her master, how horrible she was... She looks pure enough on the outside. Look at those..."

"That's enough! Here pass me that sponge. There I've isolated the liver, spleen and all their vessels. The liver first, some clamps and the scalpel... Now help me carry it over to the bath, great! And the spleen, there. I'll connect them to the machine now if you're ready?"

"She's all warmed up and humming, connect away."

"Fluid levels?"

"Optimum..."

"Great, here goes. These automatic tube grafts are really something Redveldt. They look like ordinary plastic tubes but bond instantly to any diameter blood vessel without sutures, and no rejection. You wouldn't want to suck these straws by accident. You'd have a new appendage."

"I wonder what the manufacturer would say if they knew how it was being used? I bet there'd be a rejection then!"

"Shut up. Let's see if we get circulation. Set it to slow perfusion."

"Done, it's working... normal arterial resistance, no need to add vasodilators."

"Okay, how's the temperature?"

"On the cool side but warming."

"Keep the oxygen, nutrient mix at normal levels for now so they've got every chance to be fully functional with complete cellular activity then we'll back it off and see what we've got!"

"Color is improving, looks like a success! Unfortunately though..."

"What?"

"The patient died! Sorry, bad joke."

"Yes but her blood lives on. With luck in a week or two those organs will be producing almost as much blood as healthy marrow. Normally a rare occurrence in nature but when necessary such as in anemia stemming from a marrow malfunction the liver and spleen takeover complete erythropoietic function to replenish the blood supply."

"Fascinating as always... Poetic, as in the poetry of blood!"

"...To a vampire, yes. Inducing anemia, then harvesting the product, blood, from a living blood bank, there'd be an endless supply of wonderful fresh blood!"

"Who's the abnormal one now?"

"What?"

"Nothing, where did you want her? The woods...?"

"No, I suppose the streets where we picked her up will do. We wouldn't want her to be missed and have those bloodhounds barking at our door."

"They'll be calling you 'the Ripper' before long I bet."

"Well 'the Ripper' may have been a doctor but he was no scientist. What we've done may very well one day replace the standard practice of donating blood and conventional blood banks."

"Or on the other hand?"

"What?"

"You might as well admit this method will probably only be used for the very needy few. I don't think many people will be comfortable with the idea of human organs being hooked up to machines to constantly pump out their blood needs like a dairy cow gives milk."

"Possibly if they knew the way the organs were obtained as in our case but there's always donor organs. Unfortunately we don't have the luxury of waiting around for some accident to occur on our doorstep..."

"So by the way, who is this mystery patient with the rare blood disease master? I think I've helped you long enough to be told... You must know more than the fact he's incredibly wealthy? If you can't say his name, at least let me know something of his disease. After all, I'm a doctor with a healthy medical curiosity."

"I'd say healthy would be the last word to describe your curiosity but if you really want to know I can say the experiment will benefit only the most worthy of patients, an actual vampire!"

"So that would explain his distaste for artificial blood or blood bank blood that's been stored for months."

"Exactly, stale blood would be like stale bread for him... bland, tasteless, thoroughly unenjoyable. Synthetic blood is even worse."

"You talk almost as if you were one yourself master. Could that be the reason you're able to exercise such terrible control over my feeble mind?" Redveldt laughs at his joke. The Count stares at him. "So this *vampire* must be a lazy fellow then not to want to bother to go hunting for himself, am I right? He probably likes to hire an assistant to go out and pickup destitute women and anesthetize them, then bring them back to his lair? Am I getting warm? You know I noticed when you smiled at one of my jokes before your teeth were well, different... I've always known about you master."

"That's enough Renfield, I mean Redveldt... doctor excuse me. You can go now and don't forget that body! Let's hope it's the last..."

"Yeah and if this one's a success, then we can start in on that other vampire condition... anorexia nervosa, isn't it?! I don't mind the bodies... really, I like them!"

"Yes Redveldt, so good of you to care."

"So we'll probably need more bodies?"

"Let's hope not yours, you seem so eager!"

"And I have a problem as well..."

"Yes, your necrophilia. Please Redveldt, stop caressing that girl in my presence!"

"Isn't she lovely master?"

In the Garden of Evil

"Inna Gadda da Vida, baby?"

"No, in the garden of good and evil... weren't you listening to anything I said?"

"I prefer Steely Dan myself, little brother. The Dan's the man if you know what I mean. Of course there are others, but for pure metallic effect it's the electric twelve string steel guitar. Don't you think? Hey where are you going?"

"I believe you."

"Remember that concert I brought you to when you were seven?"

"No."

"Bummer..."

"Yeah well I've got this major paper, you know end of the year, make or break situation and I'd really like to ask you about it. I could use all the help I can get."

"Okay little brother, fire away."

"What I'm trying to ask is what if suddenly there was proof, you know laid out in front of you, undeniable, irrevocable proof in the existence of God, Adam and Eve, the Garden of Good and Evil, all that. What would you do differently?"

"I think you may be asking the wrong guy about that. You know I didn't have to read the Bible until I was twenty. But then I had to read most of it practically all at once and it was very traumatic. Ha! Just kidding, but the professor was very intense and did expect some reading... I knew right away I never wanted to become a philosopher, religious fanatic, philanderer, panhandler or any of those things."

"It's an assigned topic... I can't get out of it. God and I never go to church, you know I've only been once or twice."

"I know, it's the pews, your allergic!"

"I don't know what they want!"

"I still don't think I can help you but personally I'd probably quit school, work or whatever if there was any hard proof, wouldn't you? I mean why bother? Maybe we should dropout, tune in and turn on now anyway... The 'truth' is out there, you know! 'Course I might get in trouble without a job, idleness being the Devil's workshop and all that. I guess the last thing I'd want to do would become more sinful so probably I'd just stay home more. That's not too bad is it? Does that help?"

"A little. Maybe I can find some evidence one way or the other. They didn't say what the proof was only 'what if' there was. What if I was in the 'Garden of Good and Evil' right now?"

"Gooda lucka, little brother... well, gotta go."

"Wait... That's okay I can talk to the door."

"Well go-ahead... I'm listening."

"What if I could have anything in the entire world I wanted! I would want material things, nice clothes. Or no, I'd want Eve first, then clothes."

"Right, lusting after some ancient chick... Is she another one of those vampires you're always reading about?"

"I guess if I received what I wanted that would pretty much be proof that God exists, that the garden exists, that I... was an existentialist?"

"I think I'd prefer talking about ancient chicks, the specifics, not this seeing God stuff..."

"Soon though I might want to know why. How had I been created? Had it taken me millions of years to evolve from a primitive life form or was it true I had been created in the image of God himself? And if man had been created in the image of God why are human faces so varied in appearance where all other animals look similar to each other?"

"You lost me, I thought it was the other way around!"

"Is the proof that God exists the fact that Adam sinned by wanting to be intelligent, eating from the tree of knowledge? The most basic knowledge would be that it's a turn-off to mate with someone who looks just like you, say a sibling?"

"So they were kicked out for having incest? Makes sense, that's pretty disgusting..."

"The only concrete proof we have of the existence of the 'Garden of Good and Evil' is that we are no longer allowed entrance to it. That's not much proof at all, is it?"

"It's a sinful place and better off closed."

"If there had been no sin maybe God would've stayed in the background? Or is the fact that mankind today is for the most part an intelligent species telling us that yes, somewhere in history our ancestors ate magical divine fruit that contained the 'knowledge of God'. In the objective sense that might mean that eating fruit is healthier than eating meat since killing is usually a dangerous proposition and especially if killing involves murder of other humans or cannibalism. Knowing who or what species is appropriate to kill is then the lesson imparted by the tree... or perhaps that one might be forced to scamper up a tree if one guesses wrong and attacks a species that decides to fight back."

"From sex to murder. What's next, vampires?"

"And what about *vampires*, what role did they play in the 'Garden of Good and Evil'? Evil obviously, but they are neither man nor animal. Are they immortal man-like creatures, maybe even fallen angels? Or might they represent some sort of missing link between animals and the near immortal long lived humans described in Genesis as of the offspring from the day of Adam and Eve... Of course God denied that man has any direct connection to the animals, but then he's been upset with us since the beginning hasn't he?"

"I guess He is if He knows how often you skip church."

"Vampires have been lurking in the background of human history to remind us that one day God may just loose patience with man altogether and decide on some animal, maybe a wolf or bat or creature of the night to receive the 'favored status' of highest life form..."

"Vampires... Sure, why not? Hey they're already older, smarter, stronger... like me. So why not the favorite?"

"Yeah, you ever think that may have already happened? Look at the example of Noah, God could have easily changed his mind then if He wanted to, couldn't He? Then of course came the saving grace of Jesus to reinstate 'man' as His favorite. So the vampire recoils to his lair to meditate and reflect on his condition. But when consumed by an irresistible driving force to feed, he strikes and claims his victim's blood. Thus he perpetuates himself through countless generations throughout the ages while waiting closeted, hidden from the world and the light of day until such time as he might find release from the 'Garden of Good and Evil' and the serpent's kiss that it is his curse to bear... for eternity."

"Jesus, little brother, lighten up already with the vampires! You trying to spook me?"

"Here, read it yourself. I've rewritten the book of Genesis to include vampires, the way the original writers would have wanted it to be done, had they known..."

I took the paper from my little brother and read to see what he might say.

When I got to the part about vampires I had to put it down.

"How could you write about something so far fetched, so hard to believe?"

"I don't know," he said. "But it seems like I've had memories of them, dreams I guess, since before I was adopted and became your brother. Sometimes it seems like I've known about them, stories, bits and pieces of their lives, existences I mean, well forever..." He smiled revealing a good portion of now elongated gleaming white canines. In an instant I ran screaming from the room.

Then I poked my head back in and said, "Ha! You got me pretty good on that one little brother. I guess you think it's okay to do stuff like that because your name used to be... Lucifer!"

"Shhhh! Mom and Dad are home."

"But what a thing to name a kid, huh? No wonder you had to be put up for adoption... Ha." I laughed guiltily.

"I know!" He said, shaking his head. He removed his press on mail-order vampire teeth and placed them in the desk drawer alongside the fake vomit and 666 tattoo that had also worked well on previous occasions.

A Cross Word

I was traveling late one night along a desolate winding road and came upon a horrible accident. A car had been obliterated against a tree and was now a twisted hunk of metal. It's only occupant, a young very well dressed man had been thrown clear, but unfortunately not before being nearly decapitated by some flying metallic debris. He lay on his back where he'd landed near the road and was gasping for breath, his limbs jerking spasmodically. Having had medical training I knew immediately that there was nothing that could be done for him. And since I hadn't seen the accident having come upon it after the fact, by rights he should already be dead. I made a closer inspection to find that the wound completely severed the skin, muscles, blood vessels, esophagus, spine and nerves, including the spinal cord itself. And only a small flap of skin, some subcutaneous tissue and possibly a few small blood vessels remained intact on the right side of his neck. I watched waiting for him to die but he kept on breathing, gasping through both his mouth and the opening from his gaping neck wound. I did a cursory search of the car to be sure he'd been traveling alone and if he might have a CB or cellular phone though it would have probably been impossible to access had anything been there.

Fifteen minutes had passed and he continued to live. I was starting to go into shock myself that such a thing could happen. During that time I placed a reflective red triangle out in the middle of the road to indicate to any other motorists that they should stop, and go for help. There had been no other cars. When I returned to him his breathing was weaker, shallower. The futility of the situation kept me from wanting to elevate his legs but I felt an irresistible urge to move his head into a more natural alignment with the rest of his neck and shoulders. To my utter amazement there was immediate reaction in that his breathing improved, became more pronounced, stronger. It seemed so absurd I almost laughed. How could he not have bled to death? There wasn't a lot of blood on the ground but it hadn't rained in a while. A small patch of ground could have absorbed it rapidly I supposed. Or had the mechanism of shock saved the man's life by constricting even major severed arteries and closing them off? Impossible I thought, the head would need a blood supply though technically I reasoned he could be brain dead and still be alive. The autonomic nervous system could function independently of the brain if the upper spinal cord and peripheral nerves were functioning. But how could they be, there was only a small flap of skin and tissue remaining. I doubted there were any nerves of consequence still communicating signals from the upper neck to the rest of the body. It didn't make any sense. He should be dead, completely dead. I decided to search his suit jacket and was surprised to find a cellular phone in the inside pocket. I called the emergency number and had started describing the accident when he spoke which caused me to jump and drop the phone.

"Don't!" He said. His voice was very hoarse but the meaning unmistakable.

"What?" I practically screamed. I stared at him and saw he was trying to speak again.

"Please don't," he said, "don't call them."

I knelt close and whispered, "you're dying. I'm calling an ambulance, that's all. You're severely injured and this is all I can do. I'm a doctor." I picked up the phone and lightly touching the man's chest began relating the details of the injury to the anxious 911 operator. I'd only spoken a few words when the man's arm suddenly moved to grab my wrist near his chest.

"No, hang up!" He insisted urgently. He squeezed my wrist feebly but actually hard enough to hurt and for an instant I felt anger and amusement at the same time. It could have been a reflexive contraction I reasoned.

"You don't know what you're saying. You're delusional," I said.

"If you let them take me I'll die. Listen and I'll explain," he said still with closed eyes and expressionless deathly white features.

"Hold on," I told the operator.

"Hang up!" He nearly shouted, again knocking me off-balance from surprise and the grip at my wrist. I hung up. He let go of my arm.

"I'll be alright in a few days," he said, "but if I'm put in a hospital I won't have a chance. I'll die for sure."

"You're not going to be all right in a few days. I'm a doctor. Trust me on that. Recovery in these cases is measured in months, years. Getting you to a hospital is your only chance. I'll have to call." I picked up the phone.

"No," he fairly hissed at me. He beckoned to me slightly then with deathly still lips whispered, "how would you like to drive the fastest car, meet the most beautiful woman, perhaps own the most expensive gem? If you do what I ask these things are yours."

"You *really* are delirious. If the accident weren't so serious it might be funny. You could laugh at yourself, ha, but you see your neck is almost completely..."

"I know about my neck," he hissed. "You think because my brain has no blood, no oxygen, that I'm delirious. Well what ordinary man would still be alive? Have you considered that?" He paused, "I don't think so. Being a doctor, you'd know more than most that it can't be so... yet you refuse to believe the truth."

"What truth is that sir?"

"Of what I'm telling you, of course. If I'd wanted I could have chosen a million different things to tempt you, persuade you to do as I ask... things that would be impossible for you to believe. But I speak the truth. I can do these things and more..."

"The truth sir is that you *are* dying. You may just have the barest peripheral circulation and nervous attachments left to maintain life but you need urgent emergency care. Soon you're adrenal glands will be depleted of their stores of adrenaline and your bodies' reflexive autonomic defenses will stop. Your severed major arteries will open up once more and you'll bleed to death in seconds. There's nothing you or I or anyone else out in these woods can do about that."

He once more startled me to almost fainting as he visibly shook his limbs with writhing jerky motions. I immediately picked up the phone and punched the buttons. "You're having a convulsion," I said.

"No, I did that! Put the phone down and place it in my hand. You haven't let me explain!" I put the phone in his hand and as the emergency operator's voice became audible he closed his hand and I could hear the plastic crack. "There I don't have much strength but that should be proof enough. Hang up the phone!" I did as he asked over the operator's insistent pleas for more information on now static filled phone.

"They may be able to triangulate our location somehow, you know how advanced the emergency network is these days. So while we're waiting why don't you tell me what it is you're afraid of anyway. I know that sounds harsh with regards to the injury you've sustained but I'd like to know how things could be so much worse in a hospital..."

"Alright... look I'm not from another planet or anything but I'm still very different okay? You doctors think all humans are like animals, all identical in form, shape and function. It doesn't work like that for me... If they inject some food or medicine into my blood I could... die from the reaction. You see I take a special nourishment, anything else would be very bad."

"So you've had blood poisoning before?"

162

"No, food poisoning only, but if something were injected directly into my blood I might explode. I don't know, it's never happened. I don't need it..."

"Who's the doctor here? Believe me with your injury, sterilized fluids are the least of your worries."

"You don't understand, they'd discover my unusual difference, the secret I must protect above all others but what I offer to you now."

"Oh you mean the three wishes then."

"Yes, well no... Won't you help, just take me away somewhere safe? Some basement where it's dark and quiet and out of the way. In three days I promise you'll be rewarded! The ambulance's flashing lights were suddenly on us at that moment, thankfully not allowing me more time to consider the critically injured man's eccentric request.

As they lifted him on the stretcher and took it to the vehicle's yawning doors I thought I saw an expression of pure hate... I was glad I hadn't told him my name because if anyone could will themselves well I knew he would be the one.

As time passed in my practice I've told other doctors of the strange experience with the dying man, and when they inevitably ask with their wry smiles why I refused to do the man's bidding, and honor his last request to be brought to a dark cellar... I tell them I almost did and would have been coerced had he not been so cross with me. That and his wish to be supplied with what he called his food, *the blood of some living animal... preferably human.* Imagine to be able to joke like that and so close to death!

I know he died en route to the hospital for I inquired about him the next day and learned that he had expired almost immediately. They had probably only enough time to insert an IV...

My Suit of Shining Armor

"New, mind you, fresh off the designer's rack would probably run you over a thousand. I bet you wish they'd mark down used cars as much as we do our clothes, don't you?" The salesman holds up a fashionable though slightly used suit. "Special polymers... NASA stuff, the morning star of clothing. Someday all suits may look like this, a suit to herald the new dawn of the fashion industry." He pauses then says softly, "some say it's haunted!" He laughs then talking facetiously... "but only by living ghosts which are the best kind! Best to wear it at night."

"Living ghosts?"

"You know, someone's talking... and not necessarily to you but you hear them and the words all seem to have a double meaning, maybe something to do with your life, something they couldn't possibly know anything about? It happens, believe me. And like other ghosts, the *real* ones... pardon the expression, these can be good or bad. They may make you want to scream sometimes, you know? The others, the good ones seem to be a nuisance or funny, even pathetic so you don't mind 'em much. Take this suit for example. You put it on and go out somewhere, maybe a movie. You think nothing's different, you're still the same person. Then suddenly everything is different. Your standing in a crowded ticket line and everybody's talking about you,

165

maybe some like you and are flirting with their friends to try to get your attention. Maybe others treat you like some urban yuppie and would sell their little sister just irritate you the way you deserve."

"The way you're doing now?"

"I don't mean anything by it. I'm just telling you from experience. I used to have a suit like this but I had to get rid of it on account of all the ghosts. It used to drive my friends, coworkers, acquaintances crazy that is until the ghost took hold of 'em then they just went after me. Whew, after a while I was devoting all my energy to please the suit... going where the suit wanted to go, meeting people the suit liked, eating foods the suit permitted me to..."

"That's just crazy."

"You'd be amazed but there's no question the suit has got ghosts of some kind. You can feel 'em just being near it. Go on try it on. You'll feel your skin tingle then maybe a pleasant warmth or a chill depending... No, see it fits fine, just right. The previous owner would be proud to see it on you."

"You really think so?"

"Sure, and that's not some idle compliment. I knew him. He comes in from time to time maybe checking on his clothes, ha! No really, an impressive gentleman... His clothes always have the most powerful ghosts."

"Good ones?"

"Well I guess that depends on where he wore 'em or what he used 'em for. This suit here is definitely one of his nicest, probably formal wear for important business."

"What business would that be?"

"Well now we're getting to the heart of the matter aren't we, why there are ghosts to begin with. You discover what he is and there's your ghost situation settled for you isn't it?"

"I've never heard anyone talk about a suit clothes like you. I guess I'll have to take them and see for myself!"

"You'll see and then some... if you're interested later I think you may find out more from the labels. I'm sure they're monogrammed."

I was always a sucker for a salesman and this guy was one of the best or at least the most talkative. Besides the suit was secondhand though it looked new and at a great price. I brought it home. Ghosts in the clothing! If anything suggested a reason to institute a non-return policy that was it... Used goods were usually non-returnable, irregardless of psychic sequelae. This store was only trying to be a little different. It worked. Haunted clothing was a very different approach but could the salesman have been genuinely concerned for my welfare? I wondered...

I didn't have to wonder long. Almost from the moment I put the suit on again at home I felt an eerie presence. Maybe it needed dry cleaning. The fabric was unusual and I'd realized I'd forgotten to ask what it was. It would have been amusing at least had the salesman not known after having gone on about it the way he did. The material was light but resilient, and though dark had a shimmering synthetic quality that made it difficult to give the color a name. I checked the label. There was only a neat hand sown name, Mory Bound, in artistic Gothic styled gold letters. Why had he given it up I wondered? Maybe the salesman's anxiety was the result of some recent tragic demise, but then he'd have been lying... making up a story. No, I could sense, actually feel a life force if you will, emanating from the suit. It felt good. The longer I wore it, the better I felt. Maybe Mort (I don't like the name Mory) had been a dealer in exotic drugs which had somehow saturated the suit causing it to now be a liability, at least at airports?

I took the suit off and looking closely noticed some slight imperfections as if it had been damaged in several areas and somehow miraculously repaired to be almost unnoticeable. To me it looked more similar to well healed scars on skin and I could make out faint outlines of holes that may have been made by

167

knives and bullets... Incredible I thought.

The next evening I had opportunity to wear the suit in public and did so. The owner of the publishing house where I worked was having a party to welcome the year's successful acquisitions, clients or as they are commonly known in the business, writers. This was the one time during the year when we actually saw the faces behind the words that we read, proofed, printed and promoted. Of course writers need publishers as much as publishers need writers so there were always those in each camp that felt superior in some way to the other camp, and it made for an unusual encounter. This year would prove no exception as notables such as Zing, Royce, Wolfheim, Nozfur, Cleever, and Bloodloam all indicated they'd attend. They represented a diverse sampling of the modern mainstream horror market and for some the names themselves evoked horror. That is especially to those of us at the publishing house who saw to their needs. Many of us though, those of us who'd been on staff the longest, were convinced that we were solely in the business of comedy. We were the gypsies, the paid help that couldn't be trusted. And most of us believed all writing, when viewed with a critical eye, boiled down to comedy, or perhaps pathos, depending on one's mood. Or maybe I was just in the wrong business. For one day at least though we'd mingle as friends, drop our defenses and mutual thoughts of murder and mayhem.

The night of the party I arrived at the publisher's house to find he'd outdone himself with preparations. There were tables upon tables of exotic foods and wines. And entertainment lasted throughout most the evening with music, dancers and magicians. Only a man such as my boss, I thought, would hire dancers to dance at a party... I kept to myself at first and close to the entertainment until I could be sure everyone was drinking. After several drinks it'd be less likely that names and faces would be connected, particularly my name and face. Gypsies preferred to be anonymous... Soon enough I picked

168

up on most of the lewd jokes that had been circulated, and what antics had been perpetrated by which writers, and who had drunk the most. I gravitated to them.

Until now I hadn't given much notice to my suit of shining armor, my pet name. It glimmered nicely with reflected light especially outside on the patio or poolside where it was contrasted against the dark night. I was impressed and it repelled stains too, I had spilled some dip on a sleeve and a drunken gypsy doused it with a white Russian to no effect. If that business about the suit wanting to control my actions were true though I doubt it would have permitted accidents. It did remain unsoiled however, so I wondered... Here and there I felt some slight tinglings which could easily be due to the drinks or to seeing some very attractive women. I would have to break my rule and talk with them, and hope they weren't dragons in disguise, or 'writers.' Who cares, I thought... I was beginning to feel the coffee liquor myself. If I guessed wrong, alcohol would save the day, and she'd only remember 'the shining armor,' the suit.

And then I saw the most stunning one yet... definitely no gypsy. She had on a revealing blood red velvet one-piece number. She looked beautiful but sober and my suit seemed to be almost more interested than I did. I was feeling a magnetic static charge as if the suit were drifting in several other dimensions at once, dimensions I had never known. I imagined horrible consequences if I tried to fight the suit. I had only to follow its lead and surrender willingly. I reached her feeling quite different, surprised I guess but even more surprising was she seemed so glad to meet me, relieved almost. It was as if she already knew me and expected our union. We talked as old friends, laughing, making others nearby jealous... I couldn't believe half the things I said. They seemed to come out of nowhere, from the suit?

I learned that she was indeed a writer, a famous writer of vampire books who had no business consorting with a 'reader,' a gypsy, a man in a powerfully haunted suit... But here we were literally zapping flies with the electricity

169

flowing between us. She talked of castles she'd seen, her latest book, why men were so fascinated with vampirism, with her... I agreed and somehow produced a wealth of vampire trivia to titillate her. We walked around the large estate finding a quiet secluded spot near a Gothic sculpture. My eyes were riveted to her neck, supple, tender, throbbing... throbbing? Yes it was positively pulsating with life, my life... the raw, warm life I needed and must have. I held her completely in my power, the power of the suit... As I contacted her body, enveloping her, I felt the suit do its work, work it had surely performed many times before. My lips and mouth were on her warm neck, sucking, searching for... blood!

I stopped abruptly and left her there still in a trance and raced to my car. I almost felt like flying and virtually fought the suit over my decision to take the car and remain on the ground. I'm sure if I'd let the suit go off without me, it would have flown a short distance at least. I knew then exactly who such a suit had belonged to... A masterful vampire had owned the suit until it had become bristling with static forces, forces of its own ingrained into the fibers themselves! Impossible you say? Just ask Mory Bound if you can find him!

The Devil's Rain

I've never seen such beautiful blue skies as in those minutes just before dawn... the deep azure blue fading to aquamarine, like the color of the background to the opening screen of Microsoft's Windows. Then there are the light pink puffs of clouds almost as if painted against variously lighter shades of pastel blue until the magic fades and dawn erupts. The clouds grow white or gray depending and the air transparent with the dullness of morning's light. On rare occasions in the summer season low thick clouds move in and prevent the dawn entirely. And on special nights when I know the sun will be blocked out, hiding and forgotten, I try to have a little fun...

The locals call them days of the devil's rain, those days where the clouds are so dark in the morning that it seems like unending night. Whether it's raining or not makes little difference to me though, or whether the sky's pitch black, dark gray, deep red or pastel blue... as long the sun remains buried deep in its massive cocoon I can lay claim to the day. I like places where the rainy season last months and I rarely if ever need to gauge the time of day. Other vampires may prefer the northern climes where the sun is often vacant and remains hidden from the land leaving it an entrusted frozen waste... not for me. The tropic's warmth and color are my requirements... and the nearly endless supply of life giving rain. Of course life can be hell for a vampire, day or night, warm or cold, rain or no, so why not experiment? You're just as likely to see a witch riding the shaft of her broomstick against a full moon as you are a large winged form of a bat... but the night is not without its perils. Flying within the lower edge of a large cloud offers all the protection I could ask, a shapeless discolored blur in the rain... perfect. I can conserve my energy for rapid dissipation to mist or reanimation into a man when I land. So this is my preferred method of the hunt and has been so as long as I have known of it for many years with the notable exception of an episode which took place about ten years after the end of the second world war... which I will relate here.

Naturally as you've no doubt guessed from my penchant for large low lying clouds, central South America and the Amazon is a region dear to my heart. Within the jungle proper flourish many isolated superstitious tribes of people, not to mention monkeys, large snakes and strange beasts that provide a ready source of blood. And at the fringes of the rain forest, civilization thrives with its many cultural attractions. A vampire does not live by blood alone. At times though I've combined business and pleasure and snacked on citizens within the city limits though always under cover of the darkest skies. And for witnesses near enough these nights or days of the *black rain* have taken on added meanings, superstitions born and retold as I said, of the *devil's* rain.

When I'm flying in the clouds, a rain cloud especially with a lot of potential electricity, you know lightning... a peculiar effect occurs. As anyone knows water conducts electricity well and when lightning is discharged the entire cloud and neighboring clouds are for that moment fusing with and contacting me in a way I liken to a battery receiving a jump. It's quite exhilarating and fortunately not damaging. A direct hit from a bolt will only momentarily phase me but anyway there is one other result and that is the rain from my section of cloud will bleed black, momentarily at least. I suppose I lose a small amount of my substance at those times but I don't mind it as it affords me protection in times of need. And to turn to mist and mingle with a cloud is truly a unique sensation... I do not seek the earth as most vampires but weather permitting take to the skies. As far as I know the 'black rain' is the only sign. Or so I'd thought for so many years.

My reign of rain ended abruptly one rainy season however. It started when I'd learned from the locals of a small town that there were a group of men interested in the black rain, dangerous men. Being a vampire I thought the men's concern amusing but since it involved the 'black rain' I listened. It seems there were several high-ranking Germans from the war residing in the area, one was reputed to be Hitler himself transformed with plastic surgery, and the others Dr. Mengela and Goering supposedly, whose double or lookalike was killed in Nuremberg. Had Hitler really survived the war? One was suspected to be Hitler because of his nasty habit of shouting and carrying on, making frequent threats to have people 'taken out and shot,' while necessitating translation from his native tongue. The men had no weapons though so nothing came of the incidents but I had to stifle my laugh with the seriousness the local relayed the story. Two had German wives as well but they banded together at times and were even seen in public. Apparently their need for kinship and camaraderie overcame the instinct for precaution. Maybe they would be perceived strange if they didn't stick together, being Germans alone in a strange country. But even more curious was that they were interested in the 'black rain' and had been tracking its sightings, studying it... as if Hitler's own notoriely wasn't enough, he was now interested in vampires!

Questions plagued me. Did he want to become a vampire? Would he try to rule the world again, mostly by night I suppose, because of me? Was it really Hitler, how would I know if we met? Hitler was known to suffer from many illnesses by the end of the war, most of them psychosomatic, but a bleeding gastric ulcer may have been real. Had they collected samples of the 'black rain' and drunk it? The effects could only be transitory in those quantities but were they really hunting me? I decided after a while I would meet them. The challenge was too great, my curiosity too keen.

I returned to the local and told him to contact the Germans, that I had information for them about the 'black rain,' valuable information to the right people. And I left a sample in a jar I'd collected myself as collateral for the deal.

Then I waited at the prescribed meeting place two nights hence, a dark and lonely cemetery at the outskirts of a small town... only the men arrived. They were eager but cautious and spoke mostly in German amongst themselves. I managed to get in a few questions about the war and how they'd known about 'black rain.' I was surprised that the phenomenon as they called it was known in other places, places I'd never been and that 'vampires' were the rumored cause but nothing proven.

The fuhrer as they referred to him, who was now bald, and beaknosed appearing kind of Jewish really, was interested to try vampirism. It seemed cryogenics no longer held much promise now that things had gone partly wrong with the war... I agreed and easily convinced them of the prowess they'd have as vampires. I had only to morph into a large German shepherd before their eyes to have their complete devotion. The 'fuhrer' had a fondness for the breed but I bared my teeth when he attempted to approach and returned to my normal form.

I explained I'd have to first drink of their blood, then they'd do the same from mine. I told them the transformation would take time but afterwards the only thing that might hurt them would be a large wooden stake driven through the chest. We laughed and they anxiously agreed telling me of the wealth I'd receive for the service. I drank liberally from all three then let them each drink a smaller amount I'd collected from myself. They fell immediately into contortions, writhing with the pain of transformation. While they were so engaged I took the opportunity to stake them high on large vertical poles in the manner of Vlad Tepesh, the impaler of legend. I was sure Hitler would appreciate the touch, having his death associated with the true master of ignominious death and exquisite pain... if he woke in time to greet the morning sun that is. The weather report called for a rare break in the weather, fair, early clearing, no rain... ideal I thought. And if they survived I'd claim it was a prank, a little good natured hazing in the way of traditional vampires.

The next evening I returned to the isolated clearing and saw them there still, not moving, doing excellent imitations of day old corpses... Why hadn't they come to me sooner I mused? Still I didn't want to be known as the vampire vigilante. I decided to cease my cloud flying activities for a time, after all the devil's rain (reign) had come to an end. And while I love the clouds, I am a furtive beast at heart who'll always welcome the night... when it beckons.

The Bloodstone Neckclasp

Passed down for generations I had inherited it from my father who though he never wore it, commented occasionally about its unwholesome appearance. 'Garish,' he'd say, 'garish and gruesome.' 'Well if you hate it so much why don't you sell it?' was my mother's reply. 'I'll do better than that... I'll give it away,' he retorted. He reasoned that it had been in the family too long to give it to a stranger so he'd given it first to his brothers, then various cousins and in-laws. After several years of giving the odd piece of male jewelry away at holidays or family reunions, then receiving it promptly back, he kept it somewhere hidden away. I wasn't really sure that he still had it until I received it from the lawyer executing his will. Curiously it came with instructions that stated I should avoid wearing or displaying it at night, sleeping while so adorned or exposing it in the presence of fresh blood.

I'd never imagined the necklace to be so mystifying... Was it all a joke? It had to be I thought but so unlike his usual humor. No, the words were more along the lines of, 'You can't buy a motorcycle, drink your milk and be home by eleven.' They seemed just other simple rules to live by. I remembered I'd worn the necklace a few times when I was younger, once when I was very young in order to please my grandfather at a large party held mostly in the basement. I felt like the centerpiece to some bizarre ritual, possibly virgin sacrifice, and considered myself fortunate to have escaped quite unlike my sister who ended up performing all sorts of songs and dances to her thorough enjoyment and my gratitude. She was probably able to be happy because she was not the one marked for sacrifice I reasoned. The neckclasp consisted of two parts, the chain with over-sized links of gold and silver, and a similarly large red bloodstone pendant. I'd felt burdened under its weight. My head was just at the size where I couldn't slip the chain off over it, and I was too young to undo it myself. I went upstairs to try to sleep, but I only lay there feeling... garish I suppose is a good word.

A couple of times I'd seen the neckclasp with its dark round stone on my parent's dresser when I'd been looking for something else, probably the odd silver coin in the new now inflation racked post 1964 clad coin era. Being summer I was shirtless and wanted to know the sensation of the heavy metal against my skin. I negotiated the clasp easily this time and placed the strange bauble around my neck. I went to my room feeling invigorated and looking into the mirror began to exercise my arms, watching the stone's reaction to my movements. The more rapidly I waved my arms, the more my chest near the stone seemed effected. My skin seemed to thin, the ribs becoming prominent then the spaces between almost transparent, a glassy translucent blueness. As I flapped, veins began to emerge snaking their way to the surface then further down the larger arteries, then the heart's pumping itself could be seen. Finally I stopped. What could it mean? I returned the heirloom to its place and wondered at the stone's cold touch having been against my skin. I asked later if my father had been wearing the heirloom since I didn't usually notice it on my forays for rare coins, and it was probably about that time he decided to part with it. 'What do I want with an heirloom anyway, even the word is garish!' He'd said.

The third time I'd worn it, it had just been returned in the mail from some relative or other my father had forced it on. He left it haphazardly lying on the kitchen table to show his frustration with the jewelry. I picked it up and examining it more closely noticed on the back, the stone's reverse, a fine etching of a large elaborate letter 'P.' When I asked my father about it he said it was probably just the symbol for the Romanian or Turkish relative who'd worn it 300 years ago. 'What was his name?' I asked. 'Paul,' he said simply. 'Really, that doesn't sound Romanian,' I replied. 'Could it have stood for a prince?' I queried. 'Why do you say that?' he asked. 'Just a hunch, the carving style is fancy especially for back then. Do you think it might be the jewelry from a royal family?' 'What I think it is is *garish*. Why don't you wear it to see for yourself? See if it helps with the girls...' 'I guess I better put a nicer shirt on first in that case,' I said.

I placed the thing on over my best shirt and smiled when my sister and mother entered the kitchen. They recoiled with surprise, 'who's this handsome stranger?' my mother asked. 'Your son, the vampire,' my father said. 'If he's going to wear it right he needs a new suit to show it off, doesn't he?' she said. 'Vampires?' I asked. 'Your father wants you to think he was born in the old country!' was my mothers response. 'A new suit is vampire enough!' He exclaimed. My sister laughed and said, 'it looks garish!' 'Why don't you wear it?' I said and placed back it on the table. 'I don't wear men's jewelry!' was her quick remark ending the episode.

So many years ago... I thought and my father had kept it all this time. I studied it once more, it *was* gaudy wasn't it? I placed the bloodstone with its heavy chain of alternating gold and silver links back in the box, and marveled that it was still in such good condition. Apparently it had never been worn or then at least rarely, or perhaps masterfully repaired in its three hundred years. Or had my father managed to get rid of it only to be replaced by my mother later with something from the home shopping network! No, the etching of the *P* looked the same as I remembered. The pouch from the lawyer also contained a small bound book which I discovered to be a genealogy or listing of family histories, names and dates written in small script and connected by lines indicating births, deaths and marriages. I had never seen nor heard of such a book pertaining to our family. Why would it be kept secret? My father certainly liked to talk at length about a lot of things but the historical family record was not one of them. I laughed a little when I thought the book might describe some other family. After a certain point and hundreds of years who would be able to say what family it belonged to... aside from whoever held the record itself! Well if an obvious recent connection wasn't there maybe some clue might be evident.

I began to read the ledger and noted right away the dates indicated were even older than I'd guessed... Starting in the mid 1400's it traced a Romanian line with every name being almost completely unrecognizable. Romanian was most inscrutable at first glance even to the initiated such as myself. I counted it an achievement that I was even able to tell it was probably the Romanian language... with myself being part Romanian and part Turkish and all-American. I'd forgotten most of what my grandfather had taught me when he'd shown me some older Romanian books as a child. Then I began recognizing a few proper names like Georgescu, Corvinus and Drakulya... and places like Bucarest, Targoviste, Wallachia... and the river Arges... from the finely drawn map that was also there. Thinking back to my childhood I also remembered a few of the strange words like pricolici or poenari, a superstitious monster and palinca which was a kind of drink I thought, but that was about the extent of my vocabulary for the moment.

I thought to try to at least confirm what we'd already been told of our lineage. Attempting to speak Romanian had never been fun and now close to impossible after so many years. My grandfather would hardly be pleased. I knew my grandparents had emigrated and of course I was familiar with most relative's names so the record should show... but no, nothing pertaining to our family at first in the strange script. I flipped to the end and noticed strange black marks by certain entries but the last day entered was in the late 1800s which didn't help except yes, our surname Talles was plainly present in a few spots. The black marks thinned out in the latter half seeming to highlight just one male per generation, always a Talles.

The earliest entries appeared to have two, sometimes three sets of dates under a name bearing the mark. Following the marks I noted the other older names besides Talles that shared the distinction. I looked closer at the mark itself and saw that it was actually a small circle with a very stylized letter *P* within it. I then checked the pages carefully but no surname's began with *P* and similarly no names with Paul as a first name, as my father suggested. A royal stamp I thought to relay a fact of ownership, that of the necklace and the head of a royal family! That the ruler be signified as a prince was a nice touch for royalty, almost humble, certainly less garish than the title of King. From the more numerous names, those continuing through the centuries... I also recognized Tepesh, though I wasn't sure why and then I checked under the initial entries for Drakulya, and yes there was Vlad Tepes, also written as Tepesh in places. Over the last hundred years or so Tepes had disappeared and the name Talles emerged, as a replacement I wondered?

I returned to the first appearance of Drakulya, Dracul and then Dracula with the subheading Vlad Tepesh... signified by the special marking. Wasn't this the man who had been known as the Dracula of history? But it seemed such ancient history I'd thought, or even legend supposedly, that is until recently. Had the legend come to life? Could I be holding it in my hand at this very moment? I stared at the stone's face... dark yet lightened by reflections, like an Opal moon shining in its black velvet night. I watched the reflections which moved while the stone lay perfectly still. It may be garish, but alluring as well. I put it on then walked out into the cool evening realizing I'd just broken my fathers will. Oh well I thought, it wasn't the first time.

I imagined the piece selling at the famous Christi's auction house... The auctioneer shouting, 'listing one bloodstone neckclasp complete with interlocking gold and silver chain, plus notarized genealogy documenting previous owners most notably, the prince of darkness and more recently one, G. Talles & son, presumed rightful heirs. Can we start the bidding at 50,000 souls?'

I felt light headed and looked down to realize I'd hardly moved from the doorway. A dullness took hold as I opened my mouth as if scenting the air for prey, and stared blankly into space. The confusion grew worse as I pawed at the necklace finally removing it from its place around my neck and returning it to the box. Gradually I returned to near normal save for the strong urge for a large steak, preferably rare... but decided on a long nap instead. As I lay down to rest still clothed I could feel the weighty impression of the stone centered on my chest. How strange I thought and wondered why it shouldn't be worn at night? What would be the harm in sleeping so adorned? Had I only imagined removing it? I felt the room swirl around me and the walls close in... I folded my arms and stared up blankly trying to remember some important long lost recurrent dream.

Long in the Tooth

The cryogenic storage chamber had remained untouched for hundreds of years. The design used in its creation was still in use much like the life-forms it protected for protracted periods of time. It needed only the most rudimentary maintenance and energy management requirements, being for all practical purposes a self-contained, self-sufficient system of generators, computers, pumps and liquid nitrogen. Something was about to change however. The internal clock, still accurate to the second had finally signaled to initiate the thaw process and within hours the chamber opened exposing the newly revived occupant to an atmosphere completely alien for the past three hundred years. The cryogenic station that housed the chamber was one of the largest servicing many thousands and becoming larger all the time. Though most cancer and disease was now easily cured, aging and eventual death would continue to plague mankind... at least for the moment.

The station's communications center had been alerted and an attendant dispatched to see to the new arrival's immediate condition. Most thawings were manual affairs synchronized with the occurrence of various medical milestone victories, but a few relied on mere measures of time, such as this one today.

The system's filed information on this new arrival was sparse showing just a name and date of freeze without any medical information at all or even a birth date. Of course some were reluctant to give accurate age information regarding their actual lives due to paranoia for the future, such as whether age cutoff limits might still apply for life saving surgeries as they had in the past. For the most part their fears were unfounded. The attendant reached the arrival after a few minutes to find him standing comfortably aside the chamber fully clothed in formal attire complete with cape and cane.

"Ah, you've come," said the arrival seeing the attendant slightly out of breath.

"Hello, Mr. Drake... M. Drake. Sorry I only have the first initial. How do you feel?"

"Please call me Count. I feel fine I guess considering, a little cold perhaps but I'm used to that." He laughs. "How long has it been?"

"That would be three hundred years, exactly as requested sir. We'll get you over to Med Central right away."

"Yes of course. And if you would be so kind as to have the chamber seen to, a system's check... I may have further need of it."

"No problem, that's automatic..." The attendant indicates a nearby motion chair to help transport the Count. He declines.

They reach the medical facility designed especially for newly resuscitated patients. The Count thanks the attendant who then leaves him with the doctor in charge. The doctor performs a few routine tests.

"Your body temperature is the same as the ambient room temperature which might be observed in a cold blooded species and your blood pressure is dangerously low. Of course these signs could be associated with prolonged cryogenic storage, but it's not the norm... You also seem to be sensitive to a wide spectrum of light wave radiation, what's otherwise known as photosensitivity or allergy to sun exposure. Were you taking medications before the freeze?"

"No."

"I didn't think so as we didn't find anything, but you also have a degree of anemia, completely undefined which is very rare in these times as all blood dyscrasias have already been quantified. Perhaps you might be interested to volunteer as a research subject... I can't *guarantee* a successful treatment but it would give the department something to do you understand." He laughs. "They'd be very appreciative. Was that problem the reason for your decision to undergo cryogenics in the first place?"

"In part, yes. You see I've suffered from the condition known as vampirism..." Just as he says this the doctor shines an intense small light into the Count's eyes. He recoils as if burned. "Please don't do that."

"Don't worry. That's to be expected, a normal reaction after a hundred years plus nap and your photosensitivity... Did you say vampirism?"

"Yes and it was three hundred years this time."

"Do you mean you've been frozen before?"

"Yes the first time for a hundred years only. I had expected too much of the medical profession unfortunately and so decided on a longer time frame."

"I'd say, four hundred years is about the record so far. No wonder there was no birthday available in your file, the computer probably thought it was a typo and deleted it."

"Actually four hundred years is but a fraction... You're not telling me there's still no cure?"

"What? I'm sorry, I guess you mean vampirism. Mr. Drake I have to tell you honestly I know of no medical condition associated with that word. Science fiction and the old motion picture days of the 20th-century might be a good reference point. But then you'd already know that. I'm afraid there have been many sci-fi monsters to come and go since those days. Quantum Man and Quarkzilla are the latest rage. And not since the mid 23rd century have there been any hard science add-ons available to the general public along the lines of *superpowers*. You might want to see about registering with the patent office if you have something you think might go commercial, medical condition or not. Much to our great dismay, lawyers still thrive off the economics of business, especially medicine... I should know, my malpractice is through the roof."

"I wonder if you realize what you suggest doctor? Though I suppose if I'm to be cured, I may have to be studied, professionally... at some point. But that would be admitting failure wouldn't it, and submitting to the standard beliefs, possibly even religious beliefs... No, I'd prefer to wait until I know there's a cure, already in place and waiting for me."

"Well with the way you talk, it certainly sounds big, this vampirism. I admit I'd be very interested to see for myself the manifestations of your affliction, and just what has you so concerned."

"I'd be happy to oblige you doctor, if you'd be so kind as to look into my eyes, but please without the flashlight this time..."

"Sure, I don't see why not... ahhhh."

"Ah sweet blood, what drink by any other name t'would taste as sweet?!"

The Count greedily takes his first meal in three hundred years, leaving the doctor asleep to wake later wondering about his own weakened condition. He then raids a portion of the doctor's blood storage compartments before returning to make arrangements with the cryogenic section for further storage. He also leaves word that the special locked drawer under his cryochamber containing a cachet of soil be left intact and not disturbed. But he changes his mind and checks on it personally using a key he'd kept frozen with him and finds it to his satisfaction. He is then intent on leaving the Center on a short excursion in order to access the degree of mankind's advancement and so plan an appropriate length of time for his next storage. He does not relish being trapped in a world where he must exist as a vampire any longer than he has to... but after all three hundred years is three hundred years, a long time. And he would not be able to resist at least a short visit to see what major changes there may be in-store. Hopefully the new world will not be overly harsh to the likes of a vampire, such as were the early times during the advent of electrical lights, or the ubiquitous use of mirrors, cameras, religious fervor...

When he'd mentioned his plans to return to his cryogenic chamber, he was surprised the cryo attendants had seemed to half expect it. One man related how many 'new arrivals' were disappointed about the pace of science in achieving an immortality of sorts for the physical body. So after brief orientation he was given a map and told to enjoy his visit to the outside. He was somewhat embarrassed at having to use a map for an area with which he had previously been well familiar but he noted that things were indeed quite unfamiliar. Fortunately his position was constantly indicated on the map as a blinking dot as was the location of the cryogenic center. Most striking initially were the roads which appeared to have a glassy reflective surface and used by a strange assortment of speeding hover cars or crafts which also utilized air travel to a lesser extent. Street signals and signs were still present but appeared to be only holograms and fairly ignored by car occupants as if their crafts were on a computerized autopilot. The sidewalk itself was somewhat automatic, a kind of variable speed horizontal escalator in spots. He stopped briefly in front of a business's window to read the news that was like a newspaper only as a sort of a digital printout and noted the year, 2401... as if it were a routine normal non-event. Maybe in retrospect it was and he couldn't find any stories to hold his interest. Looking around, the buildings of course were different, some spectacular in design reminiscent of the silly futuristic cartoons he'd seen before... fairly wide circular bases narrowing to very thin middle sections which expanded to great rounded affairs at the dizzying heights. Maybe they'd been designed to move like plants on a central stalk in the wind, if there even was *wind*.

When he'd decided he'd just about seen enough, the Count suddenly realized he'd been walking around in broad daylight and not felt any undo effects! Had that doctor secretly cured him without mentioning it, possibly a joke? No, he had to doubt it, he'd experienced the usual craving for blood and satisfaction after. Maybe the cure would take a while to be effective, still he'd touched the man's mind. He'd have known if he'd been lying. Perhaps the entire city were within a climate controlled enclosure... perhaps. Though hazy, the sky looked as he remembered it, but that had been so long ago. If this were indeed artificial light then it must be some job to change the bulbs! His thoughts returned to the blood he'd consumed. It was almost funny how it was still stored in small plastic sacks in a glass refrigerator, as it begging him to take it. Had it been a trap? At least it had tasted the same as that of the doctor. He'd drunk at least subconsciously like he hadn't eaten in three hundred years. He'd doubt if there'd be near the need of it now - blood, in the general public that there'd once been. He felt the old paranoia, the moral dilemma of vampirism creep back in... Would his existence, his thirst, be tolerated in this new time? Would he give them a choice? No... people still had blood, still needed it when it was lost. There were simply less diseases... aside from vampirism. Why hadn't they cured it? Or could he be the last? Physically he felt nothing, no different, there were no obvious changes that might explain his tolerance to daylight. He stopped a passerby who looked at him as if he were crazy, before calmly explaining the rational basis for artificial light... In this world he knew he'd only be worse, much worse given free reign by day.

Back at his cryochamber he fights the strong urge to bite the attendant as they make final preparations for his restasis or re-suspension into disanimation. His attendant this time is a girl and rather attractive in her brightly colored synthetic wrap, making the situation nearly irresistible...

His fangs protrude awkwardly over his lip but with luck are not observed... He knows as any hopelessly lost addict his condition is far from a cure. As he enters the small space and lays down assuming a pose he'll keep for the next two hundred years he imagines the events that have come and gone, the distant changes, civilizations under stress, lost and reborn again... through it all the inexorable advance of science and yes, hopefully even medicine, space flight and the travel to distant worlds. Maybe he'd wake-up in such a place, an unwitting space traveler through time. What better volunteer could there be? He'd be monitored by the drone computers of his space craft until he crashed landed on a world so distant from Earth as to defy his ability to even perceive it. Would it be a world without blood? He wondered, a future world without blood... was that what the cure he'd sought for so long be like?

He stares out through the transparent panel at the attendant and feels the beginnings of the nitrogen's icy touch. He should call out or alert the girl to stop the process, and demand not to be put into outer space! But that would be unlikely wouldn't it and what can she do? Besides it was too late... The sedative works, he's relaxed then plunged into a welcome darkness.

Vampire Dreams

The ship rocked listlessly to and fro on the wide expanse of sea almost as if it had been doing so endlessly, its course chartered by a drunken captain, or perhaps someone not unduly concerned with changes in the wind and deeper currents that is the almost constant preoccupation of most seafaring men. A thick shroud of fog covered her bow and deck extending out to sea in all directions as serpentine tendrils of some monstrous ghostly squid whose body had consumed an entire tall sailed schooner. More accurately it lay with its nebulous massive decaying body inexplicably draped along the breadth of the ship's railings, and hanging over the bow.

The captain held our position and we observed the strange 'dead' ship for more than an hour. I, being the only other doctor present on-board beside the luxury liner's official ship's doctor, volunteered to go with a small party sent to investigate in a high-tech life boat. At least this is what the captain said of the mission which I suppose was meant to assure me. He seemed to an extent correct about the small boat as the craft moved swiftly through the choppy brine and the distance was not great, perhaps a quarter mile. The other five of my crew were not apparently greatly concerned by this sudden twist of fate in having left the comfort of our hulking city on the sea to set out in a fifteen foot motorized skiff toward what might turn out to be a secret military study in camouflage, an abandoned pirated ship, or worse yet the devil's triangle itself though somewhat traveled from its usual suspected point of origin near Bermuda. Of some comfort was that the sonar proved there were no half submerged volcanic islands waiting to run us aground.

As we grew nearer a distant creaking sound seemed to emanate from above deck, probably the result of weathering and merciless fog which was so densely situated in proximity to the ship as to be a part of it. Upon reaching her side we made a few futile attempts at calling someone's attention but the fog seemed to muzzle the bullhorn as if it were without fresh batteries or the power switch neglected, or other unspoken possibilities I refused to let leave my lips. The first mate as I called him, or the man who boarded first did so in the old-fashioned way of tossing a knotted rope with a weighted hook to the railing. I couldn't help feel as if a sudden transition in time had occurred to that of a more primitive difficult existence, where seamen sailed only by the good graces of God and upon their ability to read their course in the stars. The crew informed me that this degree of fog in such a formation at this late hour in the day and at our region of the Pacific was unheard of. I laughed and reasoned that surely God must not be at all tolerant of the goings on aboard the... whatever her name was I couldn't guess as the markings were well shielded by the cold grayish soup which actually seemed to smell like the decaying giant squid I imagined it to be.

Luckily for the rest of us the first mate found a rope and wooden step ladder which he tossed over the side. Once we were all on-board there was no sign of the first mate and the creakings seemed very loud even through the fog as if the ship were breaking apart beneath us. The mate had obviously begun to search but as I couldn't see two feet I opted to stay by the ladder and wait to be called if needed. After ten minutes the creaking lessened and I heard no footsteps or voices. I called out several times to no response but the eerie dread calm and damp fetid breath of the fog which felt cold though it was already mid-afternoon. And this on only the third day of a tourist cruise line from the southern California coast! We were perhaps several hundred miles west of the torrid Baja Peninsula of California's desert-like southern extension into Mexico. The summer heat had been intense on the main deck of the massive cruise ship where I'd been enjoying the poolside sights just moments before... In perspective I should have enjoyed the sudden chilly air but its bite was cruelly cold, much too cold to be normal, perhaps even near freezing. It was difficult to determine if my own breath was fogging now as the thick condensation was forcing itself into my lungs before my breath could be expelled. I couldn't believe how miserable I'd become in such a short time.

I called out again, this time adding a few epitaphs to underscore my earnest desire for acknowledgment. It was as if my words were swallowed by the cold vacuum of outer space, they vanished from my lips with barely a ripple in the vast sea of unsettling grayness... I made my way down the ladder intent on waiting in the boat where there was less oppressive mist and warmer air close to the tropic ocean surface. To my horror and amazement the skiff was gone, its safety lines floating on the still water. I tried to make out if the liner only a couple hundred yards away minutes before could be seen. Beneath the layer of dense fog I had an unobstructed view of the ocean's empty surface. I slowly climbed back up along the craggy hull cursing the ship as if it were some bloated diseased corpse, just the thing I'd spent thousands to get away from on a vacation from sick and dying hospital patients. I climbed back on-board deck and awaited whatever fate had befallen the crew of the schooner and now myself as well... perhaps they were only lost I prayed. After minutes which seemed like hours I saw the dark shape of a creature appearing to completely blend with the mist which was now so dark as to give the illusion of night. Was it a man or something with wings or worse... I couldn't tell. I tried to jump overboard but was prevented by the fog which held me cushioned as in some spider's fluffy snare. I knew I was doomed. I could only say, "who... please tell me!"

"I've been expecting you," he said. "I timed my vacation to coincide with yours. I can see the resemblance. You see I knew your great grandfather Dr. von Hellschoir... He tried and almost succeeded in killing me, he and that wily John Barker."

"Dracula?" I gasped.

"But now they're gone and there's no one to torment me. No one that is but you..." his horrible laugh reverberated in my ears and muffled by the fog was of a surreal dreamlike quality... He had the teeth of an animal, horrible large killing teeth..."

"Renfield!"

'snorting... "Yes, master!"

"Wake-up. You've been dreaming and talking in your sleep the way you do. When will you learn to sleep by day as would be considered normal for the servant of Dracula?"

"I don't know master."

"You're right you don't know."

"What were you dreaming of?"

"Uh..."

"Never mind, I know perfectly well what it was, I could hear every word. You could really be a narrator in movies or news... they wouldn't even need to give you a script!"

"Thank you master, now I remember. I was dreaming of you..."

"Of course you were. It was a good dream then and I was performing admirably, up to expectation?"

"Yes of course, you were wreaking havoc on an old ship. You had already gone through the crew, and were about to defeat your arch rival... or his descendant I should say."

"What did he look like?"

194

Renfield points a large movie poster promotion he's tacked to the wall indicating one of the actors in Hollywood's latest Dracula movie, and makes a motion of hammering a stake through his chest.

"Ah von Hellschoir... in that case you may resume you dream and make sure I finish him this time!"

"Yes master. Master?"

"What Renfield?"

"Well I was thinking... What if he, you know... what if that's what he wants me to do? Maybe he'll be waiting for me to sleep so he can take a sharp wooden stake and drive it right through your hear...t?"

"Renfield! Snap out of it, on second thought maybe you can find something to do, and I don't mean another trip to the movies. I think you've seen that movie so often you're replaying it constantly in your sleep, and the sequels as well!"

"Yes, I know them all by heart..."

"I'm sure you do Renfield. Why don't you see what you can find for dinner? I'm starving." Renfield runs out into the night with a burst of enthusiasm eager to do his master's bidding. He's frothing at the mouth and snorting, as he searches... looking for something moving, alive, and preferably human!

Afterword

This title story of **Vampire Dreams** also serves to help introduce two of the main characters of my novel **Dracula, The Remergence of Vlad**. A story in easy to read screenplay form, dealing with the enduring legend himself, his new life in America, concerns for his image and Hollywood movie career.

Author Bio

Richard Reich is the author of two vampire books and several short story collections dealing with horror, science fiction, mystery and unavoidably humor... He has a bachelor's degree in Biology from Davidson College, and a medical doctorate from Fatima College in the Philippines. He's worked as a resident pathologist and cytotechnologist, but finds the relaxed pace of life as a writer more to his taste.

He can be found making his existence in St. Petersburg, Florida. Hobbies include the body pump style of aerobics, golf and cats.

www.ingramcontent.com/pod-product-compliance
Lightning Source LLC
Chambersburg PA
CBHW020606250626
47154CB00004B/1385